THE DERANGED

KATE MYERS

THE DERANGED

KATE MYERS

Book Cover Design by ebooklaunch.com and MiblArt.com
First Edition 2019
ISBN 978-1-7332322-1-0 (*paperback*)
ISBN 978-1-7332322-0-3 (*ebook*)

To my grandma,
you would have been proud.

PROLOGUE

"Sam, listen...I feel it in my gut. We've worked together for what, ten years?" I plead. I'm standing in the doorway of my boss's office. I watch the coffee cup tremble in his hands as it makes its way to his lips. He takes a cautious sip before setting the cup back on his desk.

He clears his throat and continues. "You're mistaken, Keith." He stiffens his posture and fiddles with the handle of the mug. "I understand your concern, but your paranoia is misplaced."

I shake my head in disbelief. Paranoia? I should be offended. "You don't trust me." It's a statement, not a question.

"Of course I do, Keith. You're the best senior engineer we have. I just think what you're saying is crazy, actually crazy. If you have some factual evidence to support your 'intuition,' then I'd be happy to consider it, but in the meantime, I have work to do and deadlines rapidly approaching."

"Fine, but I'm working on putting it all together. I wish you'd just tell me who the contract is with."

"That information is confidential. Please understand." His jaw clenches and his eyes shift focus from mine back to his thumb and finger as they caress the handle again. It's interesting the things you notice when you think something is off, that something is wrong.

I'm not paranoid.

Okay, maybe I am, but I have reason. And when I get back to my lab, I'll have proof, I'm certain.

"Oh, and Keith, Karen wanted me to make sure you were still coming to dinner on Saturday."

I manage to crack a slight smile. "Of course," I reply. "As long as she makes that chocolate mousse."

His demeanor changes, and the air doesn't feel so thick in the space between us. "I'll tell her your terms. You're bringing Max, right?"

"We'll be there."

Heading back to my lab, I feel eyes on me and scan the glass windows overlooking the workers. I see them, the eyes. The eyes that follow your every move, that belong to the man wearing all black, the same standard outfit worn by the other "mystery" men we've had here at DimChem Engineering for the last two weeks, all broad shoulders and excessive muscles for a place full of scientists.

The guys creep me out.

I make it back to my lab and close the door just as the tests I had started beep to let me know they're done.

Usually, our lab gets detailed instructions with what chemicals to use, the temperatures, all the conditions and boring geeky stuff, but for some reason, last week's order from this new company came with vials coded with single letters, and no other information detailing the contents.

I shift my focus to the report on my screen and instantly feel a mix of satisfaction and fear that I was right. My stomach begins to churn as I hurriedly scan the details. *Noted to be categorized as a single cell organism...mind-paralyzing effect... flu-like symptoms when ingested...blacklisted and deemed bio-weapon...not to be used with XXX and XXX.* Numerous sections of the report are redacted but I have enough, I know this will be enough.

I take a deep breath and print the report out. I have to take this to Sam. This is what he wanted, he wanted me to find proof to back up my gut feeling. Something is wrong, and it has to do with those mystery men with menacing looks and their lips pressed in tight, emotionless lines.

I grab the full report from the printer and walk briskly back down the corridor to Sam's office. I can't help but check over my shoulder, and I see the mystery man pressing his index finger against his earpiece and talking into his lapel mic.

After a few moments, I round the corner to Sam's office. His door is closed, and the lights are off. Strange. He was just there a few minutes ago.

I knock. No answer. I knock again and test the doorknob to confirm it's locked.

I put my face up to the cold glass of his office window and peer into the darkness inside, but I can't make out anything.

I reach for my wallet and pull out my AAA card as I look behind to see if anyone is watching. The coast is clear, and maybe only temporarily. The guy that was eyeballing me must be close. I shove the card between the door frame and door handle and wiggle it until it's just above the lock, praying this is one of the kinds of doors this will work on, like in the movies. I continue to wiggle the card and move it down until I hear it: the lock breaks free, and the door springs open.

My heartbeat thumps in my ears, and I swallow hard before I call out quietly: "Sam?"

I make my way around his desk, and the pit in my stomach grows deeper.

He's face down at his desk, motionless.

No, no, no. "Sam?" I shake his shoulder gently, then more urgently.

My fingers make their way to check for a pulse, and I'm so overwhelmed that I could vomit. I feel the urge rise in my throat, but I swallow it down and regain my composure. I flip on his desk lamp and see, tucked underneath his right arm, a small piece of paper with his handwriting. I pull it out from under him and read: *You were always right. Take it all. Purple flowers. I'm sorry.* A code that I understand clearly.

His other hand grasps a small vial that I instantly recognize. There will be no reviving him.

He's gone. And I can't help but wonder if we're all goners, too.

I have to leave. I have to get Max.

I rush to Sam's filing cabinet and grab every folder and document inside. I hear someone say loudly, "He's in the office!" followed by the sound of doors opening and closing and footsteps. Fortunately, Sam's office has a side door leading straight outside, so I run straight to it and into the employee parking lot. Before I can even truly process what just happened, I'm speeding down High Street in my SUV to get my teenage son.

CHAPTER ONE

MAX: Thursday, May 21

School was canceled again today. I glance down at the notice sitting on the counter from three days ago. *Columbus city schools have worked together with the CDC to determine the need for a* **REACTIVE** *dismissal...many students and staff sick...risks associated with flu outbreak...depending on further severity...possibly five to seven calendar days...please follow our social media outlets for updates.*

I'm glad though, that school has been canceled—it gives me time to catch up on the homework I've been putting off, not to mention it keeps me away from all those sick people. I didn't get the flu shot this year, and I really don't want to catch whatever bug is going around before my senior trip. I grab my backpack off the kitchen barstool and make my way to the front porch.

Deacon's parents have a timeshare in Panama City, so we're renting a 12-passenger van for the trek from Ohio to Florida. We're scheduled to leave the day after graduation. Tobee and Knox decided for our group that we should do a "bros only" trip since most of us are going away to college. The decision pissed off a few of the guys' girls – one thing I'm relieved to not have to deal with. Jules and I broke up right after Valentine's Day. She kept insisting that I decide on a college so we could stay close, but I couldn't bring myself to just pick one as quickly as she wanted, so we agreed to end things. We had a few good months, but the idea of sticking together for college just didn't sit right with me.

I still haven't decided on a college, even though I was accepted everywhere I applied.

My phone vibrates and as I look down at it, a notification pops up from the local news channel. All schools in the Columbus metro area will be closed tomorrow, Friday, May 22, along with all evening extracurricular activities for tonight. I let out a quiet "Yes!" and turn my attention to my assignment, my senior English final. Well, no better time than now.

Name:

"Really?" I mutter under my breath.

I scribble *Max Sinclair* in blue ink.

I glance down the page; five questions need to be answered.

The first question asks: "Where do you see yourself in five years?"

I let out a deep breath. I can do this. This paper may be the death of me, but it's the last assignment standing between me and graduation.

If you want to know where I see myself in five years, I have to start first with where I am now. And where I am now, as I write this, is sitting on the steps in front of my house. There is a set of old, deteriorated steps off of my front porch. The porch almost doesn't qualify to be one, because you can barely fit a chair on it. My steps are attached to my neighbors—each building houses two families. Traditionally, that is; I'm almost positive the duplex at the end of the street has five generations all living in one house.

I've sat on these steps more times than not. And lately, every day. These steps were here before me, and will be here long after me. These steps are home.

Yet, I sit, staring blankly from my seat on these steps and wonder, where is home, really? I understand the concept of "home," but, maybe with my over-analytical mind, I've never truly felt "home." Becoming an adult, I see "home" not where I chose to be, but where I ended up, by fault of my family. While I am not unappreciative of the upbringing I have received, I just want to venture out and find purpose in life. I want something different. And while "different" is such a vague declaration, it's what I hope to achieve. A purpose. So, if you want me to answer honestly where I see myself in five years, then my answer is simply: anywhere but here.

If my English teacher wouldn't have made this assignment worth 25% of our final grade, I wouldn't have even bothered. She claims it's for the future version of us, so we can go back years from now and reflect on what we wrote. My dad gave me the whole, "I know you're eighteen, but while you're still living under my roof you have to get good grades" speech when I told him I didn't want to do the assignment.

I decide I've done enough for now and pick up my phone to text Oliver. He told me if school was canceled to call him if I got free time so he could come over and play COD. The blue text bubble on my iPhone turns green, and the red exclamation point pops up showing that the text won't deliver.

"Technology..." I mutter, dissatisfied.

I hit that fancy call button my dad always gives me crap for never using. The call won't connect, so I put my phone in airplane mode and back to restart the cellular network.

Still nothing. Whatever.

My irritation is interrupted when a few girls approach. One of them is Skylar—my neighbor's niece—and the other two I've seen in the hallway at school, but I don't know their names.

Skylar and I practically grew up together. Our parents were good friends growing up and had decided after college to buy houses next to each other.

I hear their conversation as they get closer.

"I really don't see how we can pull it off, Haley," says Skylar.

"Trust me, Sky," pleads the girl whose name must be Haley. "I have a plan. It's YOUR birthday, let's go celebrate!"

"Well, whatever, but do NOT get me in trouble. My uncle is pretty cool, but I doubt he would be OK with this," says Skylar.

"C'mon, Sky, don't be such a big baby," says the other girl whose name I still don't know.

All three pause, and look at me.

"Do you have a problem? Stop eavesdropping! D'you know this kid?" says Haley.

Skylar looks at me and responds, "I don't know," then turns back to the other girls.

"Whatever, I'm leaving. I'll call you later with details. I'm picking you up tomorrow even if it's against your will." Haley turns to the other girl. "C'mon Megan," she demands and then turns to walk away.

I glare at Skylar. "How do you 'not know who I am'?"

And yes, I used air quotations with my fingers to emphasize my point.

"It's not like I even remember your name. What is it?"

At the beginning of my third-grade year, her fourth, Skylar's parents decided to separate. Her dad drank too much, and her mother carried her resentment on her sleeve. They sold their house to her uncle and moved to separate sides of town. She ended up going to a different grade school, and by the time we got to high school, she didn't even acknowledge my existence. I would have been okay with it, I mean her not wanting to be friends, but she purposely acts as if I'm a complete stranger to her, and I'm clearly not. Our moms were best friends, which meant Skylar and I were together nearly every day until the separation.

Skylar is the girl who hangs out with those fake girls, the ones who wear too much makeup and date college guys. It's all out of place though, because she's not one of them—she always seems to have the right amount of makeup on, if any, and I never heard of her dating anyone. She also seems to have common sense, which the other girls lack massively.

Last year we took an AP math together, and she never failed to answer a question correctly when called on by Ms. Summers who, I swear, got her rocks off on trying to humiliate her students by randomly calling on us to answer nearly impossible questions. But for some reason whenever Skylar was out of that classroom and around her friends, she put up a front that highlighted how narcissistic she could be.

Every few weeks she comes to visit her uncle.

"Max, the same name I've always had, Skylar," I say to her.

"Pretty sure that's Sara's dog's name," she says while looking at her phone.

I can't help but just shake my head.

This girl is the most frustratingly beautiful person. Part of me resents that she's completely oblivious to the feelings of those surrounding her. And the other part of me is completely captivated by her dirty blonde hair and bright eyes.

Instead of arguing with her about my apparently unappealing name, I ask her, "So what's Haley planning that's gonna get you in trouble?"

I honestly didn't even think she was going to humor me with a response but she replies, "It's not my plan. Haley's tryin' to get fake IDs so we can go to a bar tomorrow for my birthday. Guess she knows a guy who's good at making them. I told her I'm fine with just throwing a party here, but she's insisting. Wiley leaves in the morning for business so I'll have an empty house until Tuesday."

She pauses for a moment and shifts her gaze from her phone to the ground. "I just don't get her. She's always doing dumb shit like this that could get her in trouble. I'm turning nineteen, it's not a big deal."

This surprisingly responsible answer actually catches me off guard a little. Maybe she isn't as utterly unaware of consequence as I thought.

Before I can continue our conversation, her uncle Wiley pulls up in his Toyota Corolla and jumps out almost immediately to greet us. I've known Wiley my whole life, so he feels like an uncle to me, too.

He ruffles my hair with his hand as he hops up the steps and says, "Hey, Max."

He turns his attention to his niece. "Skylar, I'm so glad you're here to house-sit, and"—he pauses with a smirk—"how *convenient* it is that your birthday is this weekend."

She giggles and hugs her uncle. Before her back turns to me, I see a slight blush run across her face and a smile that immediately makes my heart race. If I didn't despise this girl so much, I would have pursued her by now.

Skylar and her friends are the type of girls that everyone loves to hate, like *Mean Girls* in real-life, just more subtly, and Skylar is their Queen.

Wiley turns to me and asks, "Has your dad heard anything about what's going on? I saw all the schools were canceled again, and half of my coworkers didn't show up today either."

I guess I'm not surprised to hear that—the news coverage on this bug has been pretty nonstop, and clinics and hospitals are reported at capacity. Yesterday, I watched helicopter news coverage of a fight breaking loose in front of an urgent care downtown. It's been at least two weeks since the coverage started. I assumed by now it would have been under control, but apparently the virus spreads quicker than it can be treated and contained. I don't know why he would think my dad would know anything more than the common folk, though.

I tell him, "I haven't heard anything, but he should be home in about an hour if you want to talk to him."

"Yeah I'll catch him when he gets home, buddy, thanks." He looks at Skylar. "Want some lunch?"

She nods and smiles back.

Right before she walks through the door, I catch a glimpse of her turning around to look at me. What the hell was that about?

I continue to sit on my treasured steps. I've been listening to Slipknot through my headphones and doodling bizarre, dark faces on a notepad where I should be writing this paper. I need to *finish* this paper instead of letting it be the death of me. The whole senior project thing is complete bullshit if you ask me. How are we supposed to write some wonderfully insightful paper about our future when we have no friggin' clue what the future has in store? I haven't even decided on a college yet.

Overtop my music I hear a commotion at the end of the street. Probably a domestic dispute between the neighbors. The sun reflects off of my cell phone screen and blinds me temporarily, so I shove it in the pocket of my jeans.

I hadn't noticed that Skylar had come back outside and has been sitting almost next to me snacking on what appears to be a handful of M&M's. Because our houses are conjoined, my steps are her steps.

I look over, and her expression makes me think that something may be bothering her, but I've never truly been able to read this girl. She continues to blankly stare at what seems to be nothing.

Blake told me that once Skylar had knocked her notebook off her desk in Trig and she never even acknowledged him when he picked it up for her. And another time, I overheard her and her friends talking about how pathetic all the freshman girls were and how they were going to ask them if they were on welfare. Who even thinks of shit that cruel? Not to mention, the whole hasn't-acknowledged-my-existence-until-now thing she's been winning at.

I ask her if she's okay, and I get the typical-girl response: "Yeah."

I may only be almost nineteen years old, but I know when a woman says she's just okay, she's probably not. My mind shifts back to my freshman year when I tried to talk to her during lunch, and she wouldn't even look at me. Maybe it was her sophomore-mentality, but she didn't care that she made me look stupid—she literally acted like we had never met and that I wasn't there. I decide that whatever is bothering her now simply isn't my problem, so I go back to my doodles and music.

A few minutes go by, and I glance over again. Her eyes meet mine, so I give her what I think is an inviting look, but she snaps at me and says, "Just leave me alone, Max. Can't I just sit here?"

"Yeah, fine, sorry. I was just making sure...relax."

"I'm fine. Let it go. If I wanted to talk to someone, it sure wouldn't be you."

I grow irritated at her response. "What's your problem with me, anyways, Skylar? What have I done to you to deserve this bullshit attitude you give me? I was just trying to have a conversation like normal human beings, but apparently you're incapable of that."

My voice grows stern and annoyed. Maybe it's not me; maybe this is how she treats everyone.

She starts to speak again, but before she can get whatever she's about to say out, I cut her off. "Shut up Skylar. I officially don't care to hear a single thing that comes out of your mouth anymore. You're rude, self-centered, and have zero compassion for anyone other than yourself. You're a textbook narcissist. You realize that, right?" I continue to look her straight in the eyes.

I hadn't heard my dad pull up, but he starts walking up the steps and interjects, "Whoa, whoa whoa! Guys, stop arguing. I don't know what's going on, but Max, what I just heard come out of your mouth was completely unnecessary." He points at our front door. "House. Now. Up, up. Go, go," he says as he pushes me up off my butt and through the door.

I hear Skylar say, "Thanks. But, hey Keith..." She clears her throat. "If you have a minute, Wiley wants to talk to you."

"Okay, tell him I'll be over in a minute."

As Dad shuts the front door behind him, he asks, "What was that about?"

"I was just telling her the truth."

"Maybe you should sugarcoat it next time," he says, hanging his keys on the hook by the door. "Max, that was a bit much."

His eyebrows furrow and the look he gives me radiates disappointment.

I mutter, "Whatever, Dad."

"Fine, I'll stay out of it. Just try to go easier on her next time. I'll be right back; I'm going to see what Wiley wanted."

He walks back out, and I hear him knock on their door. Thinking about what I said to Skylar, I wonder if I was too hard on her. Then I wonder why I care. I hear their muffled voices on the front step, so I stand by the front door to hear what they're saying.

"But why do you think it's spreading so fast?"

"I don't know, Wiley. I know just as much as you."

"Okay..." He adds, "I just assumed you might have gotten a memo or something at work."

My dad chuckles. "They really don't inform the engineers much of anything, let alone something like this. They haven't posted any information about this at all, actually."

He pauses, and when Wiley doesn't say anything he adds, "Just make sure you're taking care of yourself. Avoid anyone if they're sick, okay?"

"Yeah, okay," he responds in a dissatisfied tone. "D'you think they'll have school next week? Isn't graduation coming up?"

"Yeah, on the thirty-first. They'll probably get it under control over the weekend. Take care of yourself, okay, and don't hesitate to let me know if you need anything."

I quickly back away from the door and pretend I've been looking at the magazines sitting on our coffee table.

"You're a horrible spy, you know?" he says as he comes into the foyer. Really though, it's just a two-by-two tiled floor where we pile our dirty shoes.

I squint my eyebrows as to show my confusion, and he says, "I could see your shadow by the door when I was outside."

Oops.

"So, you really don't know anything? Or you're just not telling Wiley?"

"Wiley is on a need to know basis, and there's nothing he needs to know right now. He'll overreact, it's just how he is."

"So you do know something?"

"Nothing definite, just making speculations."

He quickly changes the subject. "What's for dinner?"

"Now I'm on a need to know basis too?"

"I just don't have anything solid to tell you right now." He does it again. "Pizza?"

"Fine," I say with disappointment lingering in the air. Dad and I have always been close, but since Mom died, we're all each other has. We talk about everything, and we can usually pick up the stuff that doesn't even need to be said. It's...odd...for him not to tell me whatever he *thinks* may be going on even if he doesn't know for sure.

After several failed attempts to call the mom and pop pizza place a couple blocks away, we decide to make tacos instead. That place should really invest in call-waiting.

I lie awake for a while before falling asleep. My mind can't decide whether it wants to think about my spat with Skylar, or what my dad is hiding from me. Instead of thinking at all, I just grab the headphones off of my desk and thumb my way to Spotify on my phone, letting the sound of another Slipknot song carry me away.

CHAPTER TWO

MAX: Friday, May 22

My day started and continued like every day so far this week. Each day has begun to run into the next. After a late breakfast consisting of a frozen sausage, egg, and cheese sandwich and a banana on the verge of being too ripe, I grab my notebook and headphones off the table by the door. I look down at the open page on my way out the door, the second question waiting there: *How do you define success?* I take a seat on my steps.

Instead of answering the question, I drift off to daydream land. The sun poking out from behind the almost afternoon clouds is a friendly reminder that warm weather is on the horizon; summer will be here soon enough and maybe it will be time for all the spring rain to come to a stop. Across from me, Mrs. Santos is shaking a rug into the street while her daughter pulls at her pant leg and raises her arms to be picked up. When we make eye contact, I wave and her prematurely wrinkled face forms a smile. I hear her other two children yelling at each other from inside her house and wonder when the last time she slept was. She's probably been hoping school would have been in session, so she could have a break from motherhood for at least a few hours.

I hear chirping, and I locate a nest in the tree about ten feet away from my house. The same type of tree is planted along the sidewalk every so many feet on both sides of the street along with street lamps alternating between them. I see little beaks popping up and down in the nest as a bird comes to their rescue with a mouth full of regurgitated lunch.

The birds hold my attention for a little while until Skylar walks up. Her petite figure draws my attention, but as we make eye contact I remember yesterday and look away. I shut her out and go back to doing nothing.

She surprisingly interrupts and says something that I don't hear, so I pull the earbud out of my right ear and respond, "What?"

"Nothing, never mind."

"Um...okay."

I slowly begin to put my earbud back in but stop when she says, "Do you ever just feel like you're missing something in life?"

I take the other earbud out and turn my attention to her after her unexpected existential question.

"It's stupid, right? To think like that?" She pauses. "Like, you're not where you should be and you're not sure where you even want to be. With, like...everything."

I haven't been able to take my eyes off of her since she started speaking, but she still remains with the same blank stare, looking at what seems to be nothing. Her soft features begin to harden as she remains in deep thought. Her lips part just slightly as she takes a long breath.

"That's my mindset every day," I reply.

"Really? But we aren't supposed to know yet, right? I mean we're barely adults. We don't need to have it figured out yet," she says, but I'm unsure if she's questioning herself, or me. Her breathing becomes erratic, and she places her hand to her chest.

"Are you okay?" I ask.

"Yeah," she responds in between deep breaths. "This just happens sometimes. I'm fine, really."

She takes a few short and choppy breaths with her hand still pressed against her chest.

I stand up, placing my hand around the small of her back and grabbing her arm to stabilize her. She smells like a mix of lemon and lavender. "Here, you should probably just sit down. Do you have an inhaler or something?"

"No, it's not asthma."

She lets me help her sit down and then focuses on her breathing for a minute. I watch her intently. She breathes deeply in through her nose, then purses her lips to slowly exhale every bit of air from her lungs.

She regains control over her breathing and says, "Anxiety."

We start to talk—slowly at first, but then we open up about the pressures of life. Friends, decisions about college and career paths, happiness, or lack thereof. I mostly listen, and she stares blankly while she talks. I'm thrown off by this incredibly in-depth, mature, conversation. She's this breathtakingly beautiful girl, and she captivates me with every word. Five minutes ago, I assumed she was the most self-centered person in a 50-mile radius, but the more I think about the way she's acted, the more I think it's because she conformed too much to the personality of the friends she's surrounded herself with. This girl isn't as one-dimensional as I thought. She is as complex, confused, and adrift as I am.

We're in the depths of the best conversation I've had with another soul in quite some time when I hear tires screeching around the corner. Alarmed, we both jump up and see my dad's Audi Q7 blazing down our street. He slams on the brakes in front of our house and almost before the SUV comes to a complete stop opens the door and jumps out. His urgency puts me on high alert.

Skylar, with a confused and rushed tone, asks, "Keith, what's wrong? Are you okay?"

My dad, almost out of breath, says, "Sky, go get Wiley, tell him I said you guys have five minutes to pack up whatever you need and stuff it in a backpack. We need to leave. Now."

She looks at him dumbfounded. "What?"

He ignores her and continues. "I don't know when we'll be able to come back, so make sure you grab whatever you absolutely can't live without."

He raises his voice. "This is not a fucking drill. Hurry!"

"Ok, ok, stop yelling, I'm going!"

He turns to me and says, "C'mon Max we need to—"

I cut him off. "Dad, what the hell is going on?"

He immediately replies, "Max, you need to trust me right now, we need to get the hell out of dodge. I'll explain on the way to our cabin. We need to move, NOW!"

I've never seen my dad act like this before, so I decide I shouldn't second-guess him anymore. I immediately run back inside, grab my backpack that's sitting by the couch, dump out the school contents onto the living room floor, and start shoving stuff in it.

At first, I have no idea what to grab but quickly create a list of necessities in my head: some clothes, toothbrush, cell phone, pocket knife, portable GPS, watch, boots. I'm trying to rack my brain on what else to bring when my dad enters my bedroom with two pistols.

I guess I shouldn't be alarmed because I grew up around guns, shooting them at our cabin, but I didn't realize this type of urgent trip meant firepower protection. We exchange looks, and because I know he doesn't want to talk right now, I just grab my Smith & Wesson M&Pc 9mm and holster it to my side. He does the same with his Glock 23 Gen 4.

We exchange another look—almost a nod of approval—and I grab my backpack and head for the door.

On my way out the door, a picture frame on our mantel catches my eye. I run back and rip out the last photo my mother and I took together before she died. I shove it in my backpack and walk out onto my beloved steps for what feels like it could be the last time.

As my dad checks his watch for probably the um-teenth time, he hollers inside Wiley's place, "Guys, hurry up!"

Wiley's muffled voice sounds confused as he tries to communicate through his house to my dad. My dad doesn't reply other than to urge him to hurry.

Skylar enters the doorway and takes me by complete surprise. She's changed her whole outfit. She's changed out of her girly pink shirt and bell-bottoms and into a faded grey loose t-shirt with dark, tight blue jeans. To top—and bottom—it off, she has on a black and white trucker hat that she threw on backward and a pair of black classic Converse sneakers. I thought this girl couldn't get any more attractive, but she just proved that wrong. Like, say someone forced me to choose a girl —one specific look and that would be my dream girl—in this very instant Skylar would check every single box. But, looks aren't everything, right? I still need to keep my guard up against her. No matter how absolutely perfect she appears to be at the moment, one deeply personal conversation about our lives doesn't change the way she's treated me and everyone else in the past.

I try to change my mindset, so I rudely ask, "What took you

so long? Update your Facebook status or did you have to put makeup on, too?"

She promptly replies back, "As a matter of fact, Max, I didn't. But maybe next time you should focus on your own personal hygiene."

As she walks by she flicks a wisp of hair that was hanging over my eyebrow. I haven't had it cut in nearly six months.

I guess she wins this one for getting under my skin.

Wiley chimes in, "Will you guys stop arguing? We have more important things going on. Speaking of more important things, will someone tell me what the hell is going on?" He directs this last question to my dad.

My dad just continues to push us all into his SUV without saying much. He jumps in the driver's seat, with Wiley shotgun and Skylar and I in the back with all of our backpacks. As we speed away, a large black SUV barrels onto our street the same way my dad did a few minutes ago. Just as we're almost out of sight, the SUV stops in front of our house and four men jump out.

Because of Wiley's reactions thus far, I decide not to mention the black SUV or the men who approached our house. I look to Skylar and see that she also saw the men, so I press my finger to my lips. She nods in agreement.

I try to wrap my head around what may be going on as we speed through the city, down alleyways and side streets. I glance up just as we run through a red light and realize we haven't stopped at any stop signs, either.

Wiley speaks up. "Keith, I'm supposed to be leaving for business in a couple hours. Talk to me."

Between navigating his way through the city, my dad responds, "I will, hold on."

I make an effort to think about every aspect of this situation.

My dad rushed home from work about an hour before he normally does. I don't know what type of circumstances would push an engineer of a lab company to such extremes. Why would we need to flee our homes to our cabin in the Hocking Hills? Why did we only have five minutes and why do we need pistols? And who were those men in the SUV? Really though, what the F is going on?

My thoughts come to a crashing halt as we make a sudden stop at a set of office buildings. I've been here before—a while ago when my dad was new at his company and they had him working a desk job before his big promotion to lab engineer.

My dad jumps out. "Max, stay alert. I'll be back in less than two minutes."

Before I can ask him to clarify what I should be alert of and what in the heck he's doing, he rushes toward the building. He grabs a decorative rock out of the flowerbeds and throws it through the front glass. I swallow the lump that forms in my throat.

...77, 78, 79...

I count in my head, and as I get to 80, my dad jumps back through the window he had just smashed carrying a big rolled-up set of papers. I see his facial expression go from reluctant to concerned as his gaze turns to our rear. The same big black SUV roars to a halt behind us as he gets within a few feet from our vehicle, but only two men exit. I assume that the other two stayed behind at our house in case we came back. Before I can even comprehend what is going on, my dad pulls the Glock out of his conceal holster and rapid fires to shoot both men in the legs. They both fall to the ground and moan in agony.

I am completely dumbfounded, the sound of the shots ringing in my ears.

"What. The. Fuck," Wiley says.

Dad climbs into our SUV like shooting two men with pinpoint accuracy is an everyday thing for him. He throws the paperwork past Skylar and me into the back. As soon as I'm jolted by the acceleration of our vehicle, I hear another gunshot and instinctively grab Skylar and duck. We cower in the back seat until I know we are a couple blocks away. As I look up, I see that there is a bullet hole in the back glass. My brain runs ahead of me, and I quickly turn my attention to the front seat because I've realized that Wiley hasn't spoken since his alarmed WTF moment, and I think that maybe the bullet that made that hole hit Wiley. I grab his arm, and he reluctantly looks back at me; he hasn't been shot at all, he's just in shock from this entire situation.

So much for not telling him about that SUV at our house.

Wiley isn't the only one in shock. I may be handling things differently than his pale-faced petrified self, but I am completely blown away by the past hour. I'm shocked to realize I don't know my own father at all. He broke into a building, stole something, and then shot two men. So much for my boring reality of sitting on those pathetic steps. Life has just changed.

I don't know who I am, I don't know who Skylar is, I don't know my father, and I have no idea why men with guns are forcing us to flee.

My dad has been attempting to fill us in on the current events and between the erratic driving and his jumbled speech, I come to understand a group of people in all black uniforms have been monitoring the engineers at the company he works for, DimChem. DimChem is basically just a chemical engineering lab, or at least that's what I always thought. They work to come up with different genetically modified products per order that other companies request.

He says he noticed that the men were very insistent about their presence in the labs and that his boss didn't seem to want them there. Once or twice a day, what seemed like the person in charge of the men would come in to the lab and go into his boss's office for around a half-hour. Each time the man left, his boss looked more and more distraught. The work at the lab had also changed drastically.

"I guess I just had a weird gut feeling, so I started taking samples of my own to test," he admitted.

"I won't bore you with all of the details, but today the samples I tested came back positive for a mind-paralyzing chemical that's so toxic, it's considered a bioweapon. When I went to talk to Sam, my boss, about it, I found him at his desk. Dead."

I guess a dead boss made him realize immediately that this threat was immense, so he grabbed the paperwork from Sam's office and hauled ass back home. Frantically skimming the paperwork on the way home, he saw that the chemical had been being put into our water supply over the last two weeks. He told us that the men were trying to get to him at the office. Probably those men in the SUV that my dad shot.

Now I understand why my dad insisted on weapons and getting out of there as quick as possible.

"This is serious, guys." He clears his throat. "And gal, sorry."

After flashing a half-smile at Skylar, he continues. "I don't know the intentions of whatever these people are trying to accomplish but we can't sit around at ground zero and wait to find out. We'll be safe at the cabin. It's far enough off the grid that I figure we can maybe ride this out until the authorities have maintained control of the situation."

I can't help but stare out the windows of our SUV at the chaos developing throughout our city. It's like a montage from a movie when everything goes wrong in slow motion and fast forward at the same time. Every few blocks I see multiple cars crashed together. One man, who appeared to be in his early 40s, was violently beating another man, who I assume crashed into his car. I saw a woman walking alone, as if today was any other day, but acting lethargic and emotionless. Maybe she was lost, or confused, or had just witnessed something terrible and was in shock.

"Can't we call someone?" Wiley asks.

"There's no lines to call from, Wiley, cell towers are down. Which concerns me that whoever they are may cut off our emergency systems. That's why I got that paperwork. They're compromising infrastructure, so we need to get around it before we're trapped."

My dad starts and stops multiple times as he tries to explain what he knows about the situation as he buzzes in and out of traffic; sometimes cars, sometimes people. I try to listen to him but my hearing is constantly shut down by my mind as the chaos of the city unfolds outside my window. We speed through the city as quickly as my dad can manage.

We're forced to slam to a complete stop as a truck and small car collide right in front of us. My dad officially stops speaking and throws our SUV in reverse. As we all turn around to look out the back window, I hear a loud thud and see a large man, middle-aged starting to bang his fists on the back of our SUV. I'm so close to him that I can see his overly dilated pupils as he continues to violently bang on the glass. At first, I think he may be desperate for help, some type of aid for the cuts and bruises all over his arms, but then I realize, his wounds are no one's fault but his own. Low, inhumane grunts escape his diaphragm, and his eyes have both begun to hemorrhage.

This man is deranged. This man wants to hurt us. This man is out for blood.

CHAPTER THREE

MAX: Friday, May 22

Skylar folds her arms over her head and brings her head down between her knees. I realize she's seen everything I've seen. Impulsively I place my hand on her back to try to make her feel more at ease. I can feel her breathing become erratic underneath the light pressure of my hand resting on her back, like it did on the steps once before.

Before I know it, words are coming out of my mouth. "Get us out of here, now. The glass is starting to crack. I don't care if you have to run him over, we can't stay here any longer. More vehicles are coming at our left."

Almost before I'm done speaking, my dad surges the weight of his leg onto the accelerator and forces our SUV to topple over the man that was trying to bash his way into our vehicle. My whole-body clenches as the tires make their way over him. The crunch is nauseating, and I have to refrain from allowing myself to think too much about the horrible things happening right now. Part of me thinks that my dad was waiting for approval from someone to make the move that he had already intended to make. My dad has had to make a lot of drastic decisions that have hurt people since this whole thing started, and I can only imagine how it's weighing on his conscience.

No one speaks the rest of the way down High Street unless it's to inform my dad of a possible situation or roadblock. We near the end of the highway before it reaches the outer belt of Columbus and decide that we should pull over. Traffic is backed up because of the roadblocks ahead, disallowing people from traveling outside of the city. We pull off of the highway and drive off-road for about 20 yards to hide our SUV in between a row of mature evergreen trees. This allows us time to think for a few minutes and decide what to do next. My dad asks for the paperwork that he threw in the back at the office building.

Skylar hands it to him and I say, "What's on there?"

"The other paperwork, the stuff I got from Sam's office...it mentioned that there would be roadblocks if things didn't go accordingly. The paperwork at the office, this paperwork," he points to the paperwork in his hand, "tells us where those road-blocks might be."

The cabin is over forty miles out of the city, so finding a way around the roadblocks is imperative. But after checking and rechecking the paperwork, Dad realizes that the roadblock presently ahead of us isn't on the map.

"I hate to say this...but I think the best scenario is to leave the car and continue ahead on foot."

I see the panic sweep across Skylar's face, and even though I feel it too, I force myself to keep a straight face so she doesn't feed off of my own worry. I don't know why I feel the need to shield her from this, but I chalk it up to not needing another person in our group to go into shock, especially considering Wiley still hasn't said much since my dad shot those two men.

After a momentary silence, Dad folds up the papers and says, "Ok, let's do this."

We grab our backpacks and belongings from my dad's SUV. We take everything that could be of use to us, like the first-aid kit that came standard in his Audi. Skylar frantically tries a little too hard to stick the first-aid kit in her backpack and accidentally drops the bag, allowing most of the contents to fall to the ground.

As I help her pick the stuff up, I notice she brought a few extra, odd, things. I put my hand on what I thought was a book but realize it's a handwritten journal. She quickly grabs it from my hand, almost embarrassed, and places it inside her bag. She also brought a Polaroid camera, the kind that prints photos automatically. I remember back to having one of them as a kid and shaking the shit out of the print thinking it would help it develop faster; come to find out that's actually a myth and doesn't help at all. With the five minutes we had to grab things, I can't help but wonder how this made the cut. Maybe it holds sentimental value or something.

As we begin to walk out, I'm unsure of whether or not I should keep my gun in my hand, but in hopes of not stressing Skylar or Wiley, I just keep my hand readily available in case I need to quickly draw it. While we walk, my dad advises us to head east in order to get past the actual on and off-ramps of the outer belt and cross the highway instead of walking ourselves right into that road-block.

We walk for a few minutes until he says that he feels confident about our distance. Traffic is completely at a standstill, and the sounds of horns blaring and people yelling at each other fill the space. The smell of hot asphalt lingers. Luckily people are so focused on getting themselves out of this mess that they don't pay much attention to us. We pick a spot to cross, between rows of stopped cars. Almost as soon as we start crossing our projected path, we become aware of a young woman making quite a scene in our anticipated path. She walks to the car beside her and without hesitating punches her once-upon-a-time dainty fist through the glass as a man from behind the car starts to approach.

"Ah man, what the hell, girl? Why would you..." His voice trails off when he makes eye contact with her and she begins to grunt at him. I become alarmed at how similar she is acting to the man we trampled over in our SUV. Her juvenile face exudes rage.

We quickly move a little further east to another opening between cars.

"Dan, what the fuck is going on?" a woman yells at the driver of her car, possibly her husband. Other people are questioning, too.

We quickly dart through the westbound lane and hop over the concrete barrier separating the eastbound lane. I almost lose my balance as my backpack gets caught briefly on the median. Skylar reaches out to steady me. I thank her.

Just as we all finish crossing over the barrier, we hear loud groans behind us. The young woman who punched the car window has given up on her last target and is running towards us. She's flailing her arms violently, and I have no doubts about her desire to cause bodily harm to us. We're around five feet away from her when she gets caught by the barrier. She appears to not have the coordination to be able to maneuver properly around it.

"Come on," I say to the group. "Before she figures out how to get over that!"

I take off across the eastbound lane, heading toward the tree line just off of the highway, and everyone else follows suit.

Once we reach the wooded area, we walk quietly and closely together for what seems like a mile. My senses are on high alert, noticing every twig that's stepped on or bird that's flown by. Even the sound of our taxing breathing feels incredibly detailed. Yet I feel completely oblivious when my dad stops dead in his tracks with his arms out, stopping us at the edge of a field.

In the middle of this field sits a large, lit up building. Two, all-too-familiar, black SUV's lead us to think this might be an outpost for this unknown radical group causing chaos across our city, one which wasn't noted on our handy-dandy map. We begin to evaluate our options but quickly grasp that we have to choose between backtracking (losing time and putting us closer to ground zero) or getting closer to this building and trying to MacGyver our way around.

On the trek through the woods, Wiley finally snaps out of his shock, and now he has gone into practical thinking mode. He and my dad stepped away and have been mumbling back and forth to each other and drawing strategic plans on the palm of their hands using their fingers. A whirl of the finger to show the building, a couple X's to show the guards and us, and curved lines to show possible ways around.

Wiley and Dad come back, and the look on their faces makes me feel as if this arrangement is going to be more difficult than they hoped. Wiley almost looks pained, the stress of this situation settling into wrinkles in his face I didn't know existed. Wiley's always seemed so young to me. I assume mid 30-ish, but I've always been a poor judge of peoples' ages. Wiley is naturally laid-back, almost always with a smile on his face or trying to lighten the mood. To see him so distraught today is a complete change from how he typically acts.

My dad starts filling Skylar and me in on the plan. Now I

understand completely why Wiley's face showed such discomfort.

My dad says we need a diversion.

One of us will have to distract a guard, the rest of us will take him out, and then we'll be able to waltz on by before the other two have made their cross-checks of the building. Wiley chimes in that he, initially, was going to be the diversion, but my dad brought up that the guard might not be on high alert if he sees a small woman approaching.

My stomach sinks. I loathe this newfound unknown emotion I feel towards this girl. I cut my dad off mid-sentence and volunteer to go instead of Skylar. Wiley looks thankful and hopeful that his niece won't have to risk herself. Skylar looks genuinely pissed that I even spoke a word.

Skylar speaks up. "It makes far more sense for me to do this, Max, don't try to play hero."

"I was just trying to help. I didn't realize you would be so quick to volunteer."

"Whatever. You act like I'm helpless and can't make rational decisions by myself. I'm fully capable of pulling this off."

Looking at my dad she says, "Now, what's the plan?"

And just like that, her stubborn disposition erases away all the positives that I had started to think and feel towards this girl.

We discuss the plan, and it actually seems like it might work. Skylar has some acting to do to make this guard believe she's vulnerable and defenseless. She makes her way out of our shrub and tree-covered area and starts walking towards the building. My palms start to sweat, and I force myself to take a deep breath.

Wiley, Dad, and I watch from about two hundred feet away. The guard sees Skylar and does exactly what we want him to do. Skylar puts her hands slightly up to signify she's unarmed and walks to his left side. He falls precisely for the bait and turns his back towards us. Time for us to move.

We quickly and quietly make our way towards the building. We timed how often the guards make their pass around the building. We should have approximately three minutes to take this guard out and move past the building out of sight. As I watch Skylar talk to this guard, I can't help but wonder whether she's a great actress, or really good at deceiving people —I'm going with the latter.

The gap between us and the guard is about thirty feet and closing quickly, and I feel a slight tinge of comfort that he's still in our trap. My heart nearly stops when another guard opens the steel door and steps out. He catches sight of us and hastily grabs Skylar by the throat, putting a gun to her head. The despair that sweeps across her face twists at my heart. It's a look of complete terror. The guard squeezes his forearm tighter around her neck and pushes the tip of his handgun further into her temple.

I'm at a complete loss for freaking words.

Not that words seem to matter—no one has spoken since this started. Either we completely caught these guards by surprise, or they don't care what we have to say regardless.

"Easy does it," my dad says gently, breaking the silence. The men continue to remain silent.

Skylar gives my dad a pained but hopeful look and exchanges some type of nod. I see Skylar wiggle her chin under the man's exposed forearm and viciously bite down. He lets out a deep groan and instinctively loses his grip to grab onto his freshly wounded arm. I rip the gun from the holster on my side almost simultaneously as I hear the gunshots leaving my dad's gun into the other man. The smell of gunpowder, sweat, and blood fills the air. Before I know it, I've already shot three bullets into the chest of the man that threatened to kill Skylar.

My mind tries over and over to process what just happened, but I can't shift my focus from the ringing in my ears.

I just killed a man.

CHAPTER FOUR

MAX: Friday, May, 22

Life returns to full motion when Skylar's arm brushes against mine as she runs past me and to her uncle. He embraces her and almost lifts her off of the ground. My dad pushes downward on my arm, reminding me that I'm still completely drawn up and in position to shoot again.

"We have to move. We can't stay out here in the open."

My dad quickly reaches down and begins to strip the man I shot of anything useful on his person. I hear another door open. Whoever was inside must have heard the shots. Shit, of course they did.

"Max, go get the other guy's gun."

We pick up two handguns, two extra magazines each, flashlights, and their radio units. I stuff a few things in my dad's backpack as he puts the rest in Skylar's backpack. From the little I know about these types of radios, they aren't the greatest quality. The men's uniforms don't match—they literally appear as if they just threw on whatever black clothes that they had in their closet.

Before whoever heard us can find us, we take off to the tree line on the opposite side of the building. I nudge Wiley's and my dad's arms as I pass them—we need to pick up the pace. We're at a heavy run, and I assume that Skylar won't be able to keep up, but she catches me by surprise when I turn to look over my shoulder and see that she's right on my tail, barely a second behind.

As we're running, I try to wrap my head around what just happened. In the simplest of terms, I just killed a man. I don't have time to sort out what I'm feeling, and I know I need to leave it till later when there isn't a chance of armed men catching us.

But I freaking killed someone. I KILLED A PERSON.

As we reach the tree line, I force myself to focus. I don't have the time, or mental capacity, to try to process this shit right now.

After we ensure that we are completely hidden inside the tree line, we're able to slow to a brisk walk. Even though I'm still working on processing all of this, one thing I know is that I'm glad my dad reacted the way he did back at the house, or I know we wouldn't have made it this far already. I still don't understand why these men are behaving the way they are, but at least I'm with someone that's able to react rationally.

We walk for what seems like hours in silence. Finally, my dad puts his hand on my arm to signify that we can stop.

"The sun is starting to set. We should probably set up camp for the night."

With the smallest voice, Skylar replies with a meek, "Okay."

For the first time since I last saw her pained face being held captive by that man, I look at her. She catches my eyes and holds my gaze.

The pain and fear has left her face and has been replaced with a hollow stare.

She looks at me like a puppy does after it's unsure if it did something wrong. I can't manage to come up with any comforting words so I simply place my hand on her shoulder in my crappy attempt to console her. I see a glimmer of hopefulness reach her eyes as she pulls me to her and wraps her arms around me. I'm caught off guard at first but naturally put my arms around her and hold her head against my chest for what seems like the shortest second. She pulls away, and I catch a slight blush reach her face as she turns to go join Wiley and my dad.

I wonder if I have that same blush searing my cheeks, too.

My dad was clever enough to think of bringing protein bars and a few bottles of water in his backpack. We sit around on two old fallen down trees and eat our gourmet dinner. I feel the fatigue of the draining day start to sink in.

As exhausted by today's events as I am, I know I'll have trouble sleeping so I take the first shift. We have pretty good protection between these two trees and if someone were to walk by, they would probably never even notice we were here. Since it's still May, it gets a little chilly at night so we rummage through our backpacks for extra clothes to stay warm overnight. I notice that the extra sweatshirt in my backpack would make a great pillow, but instead of keeping it for myself, I hand it to Skylar to borrow.

She seems appreciative, and says, in her small voice, "Thank you."

I guess it took an almost life ending event for her self-centered entitlement to go away.

Everyone else is soon fast asleep. I assess my surroundings

before deciding to get up to stretch my legs. I hop up and slide myself to the other side of the tree. On my way down, I accidentally kick over two of our backpacks. Picking them back up, I realize that a few things fell out of one of them.

I whisper out loud "Shit!" when I realize it was Skylar's bag. I quickly start shoving her items back inside. When my hand lands on her journal, I hesitate before I realize this is my opportunity to peer inside to learn more about this very confusing girl.

I flip a few pages in and see an entry from only a few months ago. It's an entry discussing college. She talks about a girl (Ava) in class that always tries to show off all of her expensive things and how all of the guys eat it up and the girls idolize her. Then she talks about a guy who made a pass at her but was a complete jerk about it. She says she would rather be alone than with someone like that. Even though this is really feeding into the "Who is Skylar Morgan" theory, I flip to the end to see a more current entry.

I'm surprised to see, on the very last page, an entry marked today, this freaking afternoon. My heart beats a little harder, and I think to myself how I'm thankful the moon is out tonight, brightening up the night sky just enough so I can see to read.

It starts out by talking about her idiot friend, Haley, and her doomed plan to get fake IDs for her birthday. Then it hit me: today is her birthday. Well, *was* her birthday since today is pretty much over. Poor girl is one year older and gets to celebrate by fleeing to the boonies and almost being killed.

I read more.

I feel myself lost in time. Where has the time gone and what have I accomplished? Unhappiness. Life should be full of blissful, complete happiness. Right? We only get this one life, this one life to experience all that we can to fulfill our dreams... Today I was surprised to have a very in-depth conversation with Max.

We talked about life and happiness. He surprised me. I've always seen him to be this oblivious kid who never thought outside the box. I was completely wrong. Talking to him today, I felt so productive...and content. His eyes are so captivating, and when he speaks about something he's passionate about, he doesn't notice that I can't keep my eyes off of him. The way his hair falls over his eyebrow sparks something inside me."

I feel a flush run across my face as I let her words sink in and am harshly brought back to reality by a sudden noise. I instinctively place my hand on my side, where my gun is holstered and start checking my surroundings—there's movement and rustling about five feet away, and my heart races, until I'm relieved to see a raccoon emerge from the brush. I lightly kick some dirt at him, and he hisses as he turns to waddle away. I shove Skylar's journal back into her backpack and set the backpack neatly on the ground.

A few moments later, my dad stirs.

"Hey buddy, you want to give it a shot? I can't seem to fall asleep."

"You sure?"

"Yeah, that third cup of coffee is kicking my ass."

As I lie down and close my eyes, I smile thinking of the words Skylar wrote about me.

About *me*.

Someone taps my shoulder, and I roll over to Skylar's unbelievably stunning face looking down at me. She's kneeling beside me. Her eyes are the kindest I've ever seen them, completely inviting me in. She places her warm, delicate hand on my cold cheek, and I feel my body ignite from the inside. I place my hand over hers and entwine my fingers throughout hers. I close my eyes slightly to savor this amazingly pleasant moment. What is this that I'm feeling; is she feeling this, too?

I open my eyes and am caught off guard to see that her face

has changed completely. Her cold, unpalatable gaze sucks every inch of warmth from my body.

"Oh Max, you're so naïve," she says condescendingly.

"What?" I reply, completely confused.

My hand slowly falls to my side. She pulls her hand away from my face in a swift motion, dragging her nails across my check on the way down. I don't understand.

She shifts her weight and asks, "Did you get it all?" to someone behind me. *Who is she talking to?*

Following her gaze, I see another man rummaging and gathering up all of our supplies. I struggle to get my eyes to adjust so I can see him. My eyes instead focus on my dad and Wiley; both unconscious, lying lifeless on the ground by the trees where they were sleeping peacefully not too long ago.

"C'mon Sky, we need to go. I grabbed everything worth anything. Let's get the hell out of here so we can hit the next group," the man says.

I stare blankly. My mind is a fog; I can't make sense of any of this. *Hit the next group?* What next group? Why is she doing this?

"What did you do?" I manage to say.

She acts as if I haven't said a word.

"Fine, but I want you to finish *this* one off before we go," she replies to him and points to me.

Finish me off? What the—?

"Skylar, I don't have time for this. If you want it done, do it yourself."

I can't even begin to fathom what's going on right now. I'm in worse shock than I thought I was when I saw my dad shoot and kill someone, when *I* shot and killed someone. As I stand up, my head begins to spin, leaving me to lose my balance and stumble to the side. I catch myself on a nearby tree branch and cut my hand deeply. I look down and see blood trickling down my forearm. It's warm against my skin, and the sight of it makes my stomach queasy. I hear a slight chuckle coming from Skylar —she raises her arm and points a gun directly at me. The same gun I used to shoot and kill the man that threatened to kill her is now staring me right in the face. Dizziness overtakes me, and I fall to the ground.

I'm slumped, on my knees, between a tree and the most deceitful person I've ever known.

I take a deep breath and Skylar says, "Anything you'd like to say, Max?"

An uncontrollable tear slips out of my eye, and I come to the complete realization that I'm about to be murdered. By someone I've known my whole life. By someone I was beginning to trust.

I look her in the eyes. "Why are you doing this?"

The hammer clicks. Another tear finds its way down my cheek as I maintain eye contact with her.

I don't know why I don't beg for my life. Maybe the utter dissatisfaction with the last forty-eight hours or perhaps because there is nothing worth fighting for.

I swallow hard; I am going to die.

CHAPTER FIVE

SKYLAR: Friday, May 22

I'm scared—I'm scared of so many things.

I fell asleep momentarily, only to wake and stare into the night sky. I've been left alone with my thoughts for too long, and right now, all I want is daybreak to come so we can leave and get closer to wherever Keith is taking us. I trusted him to keep us safe, and he's done that, but I'm scared. What does he know that we don't?

I'm scared of these men in all black, the sickness overtaking people, the unknown. I'm scared of Max, and the effect he has on me. I feel my walls breaking down around him, in an uncontrollable way. I have this desire I can't control to be near him, in any way. He's so shut down, so closed off, and I can't help but want to know why, and to tell him it's okay to let me in.

Something about the way he resisted letting me be the bait, and the terror on his face when that man had his arm firmly against my neck, gun pressed against my temple—it changed me in a way I can't describe. I continue to process what's happening, with this whole thing, with everything before, and everything with Max, and I continue to run circles around my thoughts, not able to figure anything out.

I'm scared to let someone in, to trust someone. I don't know healthy relationships. I have Wiley, and he's always been someone I could rely on, to an extent.

I can't talk to my mom, she's changed. Or maybe I've just grown up and remember a different version of her from my childhood. She's always been tense, and heavy, carrying the burden of a failed marriage on her shoulders. Maybe I was oblivious to how this affected her when I was a child, or maybe she just reached a breaking point one day, and it all showed through on the surface.

My dad stayed in the denial phase for as long as I can remember, using alcohol to cope with his failed marriage caused by his alcohol addiction and neglect. The every-other-weekend court-ordered visitation gave me the freedom from my overly-stressed and anxious mother but meant the inconsistency of not knowing which dad would be around—the fun and sober, or the mean and drunk.

My heart beats harder in my chest and takes my mind away from my thoughts. I fight off the urge to let my anxiety overtake me, something I've conditioned myself to do over-time. In through the nose, one-two-three-four...hold, five-six...out through the mouth, seven-eight-nine-ten... I repeat these steps a few times until I'm distracted by slight murmurs. As I sit, I see Max moving gently but notice that he is still asleep.

Through the illumination of the sunrise, I see Keith and Wiley fiddling around their sleep areas. Keith motions to Max and tells me, "Will you wake him?"

I oblige and after I've made my way to him, I kneel and place my hand on his shoulder.

"Max, hey, wake up," I say awkwardly.

He doesn't budge, and for a moment I don't mind the up-close viewpoint. I study him, his face tense, creating wrinkles in his forehead peeking out from under the wispy mud-colored hair that I ache to sweep to the side. His nose curving downward, slightly crooked, but in a makes-his-face-what-it-is kind of way.

I clear my throat and shake him a little harder.

CHAPTER SIX

MAX: Saturday, May 23

Instead of the sound of my life ending, I hear her quietly, but urgently repeating, "Max, Max, Max! Wake up!" She continues to nudge my shoulder.

I jolt myself upright and realize I just had one of the most intensely vivid nightmares I've ever had. I instinctively smack her arm away and she gives me a scolded look. Part of me doesn't feel bad for my reaction, when my subconscious seems to be so aware of how falsehearted this girl is. I'm sick to my stomach with the absolute recollection of what just occurred in my mind.

"Leave me alone," I mumble as I stagger to my feet.

"What did I do now?" she asks with sarcasm in her voice. "Did someone wake up on the wrong side of the tree?"

"Will the two of you give it a break? I thought after last night you might actually stop relentlessly arguing with each other," says my dad. "We need to come up with a game plan to get to the cabin as soon as possible. Daylight's coming faster than I want, and we need to keep moving."

"Fine," I reply. I went to sleep feeling hopeful and incredibly optimistic about this entire situation, but now I don't want to be around any of these people. I pull the hood on my sweatshirt up to cover my head, and when no one is looking, I reach up and put one of my earbuds in. Not enough to take away all of my senses, but enough to try to let the music soothe my aching soul.

The plans for our next move are finalized, and we move out in less than five minutes. That allows enough time for us to gather our belongings and clean up any trace that we were here. I see Skylar out of the corner of my eye fumbling with the gun my dad let her carry. He said it was a good idea to let Skylar and Wiley both carry one, not knowing what we could be up against again. It seemed like a good idea at the time. Now, as I see her with the gun, I get a flash from my nightmare. I'm startled and sickened at the same time. I try to remind myself it was just a dream, but I can't seem shake to it.

I had forgot that I let Skylar borrow my extra sweatshirt until she hands it back to me. I quickly grab it out of her hand and shove it into my backpack. She manages to speak a swift "thank you" before I turn my back and walk away.

Before I can get far, she grabs my arm, "Hey..."

I turn slightly.

"Is everything okay? We seemed fine last night, and now you're acting vindictive as hell."

I reply, "I'm fine, Skylar. Let it go." I pause for a second. "And if I wanted to talk to someone, it sure wouldn't be you."

I make the same stab that she made at me once upon a time. I see the hurt cross her face but decide to turn my back and continue walking away. We need to move anyway, so I focus my thoughts on the sound of music playing in one ear and the sound of leaves and dirt crumbling beneath my feet in the other. It's a few seconds later before I hear her footsteps crunching across the ground behind me. Her pace is steady and consistent, so I know she's made the decision to not catch up to me to discuss this anymore.

The map my dad shot those two men over indicates there is a *resource storage building* close by. It's only about a half-hour walk, with a tiny town in between, and we decide the trip is worth the time to possibly get more supplies. I've got my fingers crossed for a set of wheels. I don't mind the walking; it's rather relaxing actually but given the situation as a whole I would much rather speed all of this up. The sooner we get to the cabin, the sooner we can figure out what the hell is going on. Not to mention I wouldn't mind having some type of freedom.

I lower my head and raise my arm at the same time to catch a whiff of my armpit. I'm in need of a shower. We all are. And damn, what I wouldn't give to lie down in an actual bed. Plus, I need to process the whole, *I'm still a freaking teenager and I just shot someone* thing. Talk about a rollercoaster of emotions I've experienced on this trip. Geez, man. I think we all need a moment or twenty to ourselves.

I try to take my mind off of myself for a second and nudge Wiley. "You doing okay?"

He kind of chuckles and replies, "Yeah, considering."

"I know whatcha mean."

"What're you listening to?"

I didn't realize any of them knew I had that earbud in one ear.

"Oh, just a little Manson, some Slipknot...the usual."

"Ahh, the screamo stuff." He smiles.

"I don't know all about that, maybe metal."

"Yeah, maybe you're right."

I feel slightly uneasy when I begin to notice houses appear

in the distance. I don't know if there are people inside, or outside of them; I don't know if they will be friendly, or complete lunatics; I don't know whether we will be welcomed, or unwanted in this town of theirs.

As we make our way towards this tiny little town, I see a sign with the words: *Welcome to Lockbourne: Population 243.* Trees line the neighborhood with a single road going down the middle and a couple small access alleys between houses.

We stop shy of the sign, still in the woods behind the town. My dad initiates the conversation. "Ideas of what we should do?"

"It's a small town, not many houses. We should be able to go straight through on the main road," I say convincingly.

"Why would we risk not knowing what's waiting for us? Let's just go around the back and through the woods," adds Skylar as she points to the wooded area in the distance.

"I, honestly, don't prefer to be out in the open, but I also don't want to backtrack and add any more time to this trip. I vote we go straight through," says Wiley.

My dad nods. "I've been listening, and haven't heard any noise from the houses as we've approached. I think we should be fine to go straight through. Maybe these people were evacuated when shit hit the fan. All we have to do is take the main road straight through, then cross into the field on the other side." He looks off in the distance, then continues. "The buildings we need to get to will be about three-quarters of a mile if we take the main road, or maybe...three plus miles...if we go around. Any other thoughts on what we should do?"

My dad seems so matter-of-fact in his speech that I assume his last question was rhetorical and we are going to do what he wants regardless. He tends to make you feel like you're included in the decision but manipulates you to do what he wants anyway. Which, who can blame him? Leadership is something that comes to him naturally.

He takes the lead, and I follow up in the rear, allowing Wiley and Skylar to walk side by side in the middle of us. My dad and I are especially observant and most able to react with a weapon, so this is the obvious choice of our formation.

We begin to pave our path into this run-down city. Town. It's hard to even call this place a town, more like a small village. The houses are nearly at an arms-length of each other. Beater cars are parked halfway into the street and halfway into the lawns. I'm not sure if this was because of an urgency brought on by our current situation, or if that was the norm here.

We've already walked by two houses and so far, no sign of life. We pass a house with what appears to have Christmas decorations still up from last year. I even see a few Halloween decorations. Maybe they haven't had the time to take them down, or maybe they just find it easier to leave them up year-round.

My watch reads 9:14 a.m., and the chill of morning is finally about to dissipate. The sun poking through the clouds is refreshing and much needed for morale. I always enjoyed this part of the year, when warm weather was finally upon us and those cold, rainy days of spring are long gone. I appreciate our beautiful winters here in Ohio, but for me, the hot summer days are my favorite. Spending time outside, at the cabin, exploring nature, that's what I want to be doing.

My eyes catch a flash of something—a figure appearing in a doorway at the house to our northeast.

I whisper ahead, "Dad!" to get his attention.

He looks over his shoulder, and I nod to the direction of the house. He stops walking when he sees her. There on that doorstep, completely alone, stands a school-aged girl wearing a pale blue nightgown and fuzzy purple slippers. She notices us and lethargically stares. My dad crouches slightly and motions for her to come to us.

He says to her, "Come here, sweetie. We won't hurt you. Are you okay? We can help you." Before he can get a response from her, if she was even going to give him one, another slightly larger figure appears from around the backside of the house. It's a woman, middle-aged, slender build with unmanaged dirty blonde hair.

My dad says to the woman, "Ma'am, have you lost your daughter? There's a little girl on the front step who seems to be lost."

My dad's speech is cut off when we hear a low groan escape the woman and child as they both begin to bolt toward us.

He screams, "Run!"

We immediately sense the threat and take off running. Skylar has enough speed to maintain a pace with my dad and me, but Wiley falls behind quickly. We dart past a convenience store and laundromat. I look to my right and see another person, but instead of chasing after us, he is lying face down in his yard.

I can only assume he's dead. We can't help him.

I continue to hear the grunts from the woman, but the child is not as swift in maintaining our speed. I turn for a second to look over my shoulder and see that the child has actually stopped running and is now wandering aimlessly through the street. But the woman is gaining on Wiley. Panting and almost out of breath, his pace begins to slow, and as soon as she gets her chance, the woman leaps towards him and grabs onto one of his legs.

Wiley trips and his body is viciously thrown to the ground. He screams out. Without a second thought, I turn around and start running toward him. The woman crouches over Wiley and starts punching him in the torso. He yells out in pain but is able to push her back slightly. He takes the opportunity to take his other leg and kick her in the chest, stunning her and throwing her back a few feet off of him. He sits up quickly and scoots back.

My dad and I reach Wiley at the same time. I grab him from behind under his arms and try to pull him onto his feet. He's heavier than I thought. The woman regains her balance and lurches towards us, but before she can do any more damage, my dad pulls out his gun and shoots her in the knee. She falls back to the ground and screams loudly, not a scream of pain, but of frustration and anger. Skylar finally reaches Wiley and helps me pull him to his feet. A painful moan reaches his lips when he applies pressure to his foot. We each throw one of his arms over our shoulders and turn to look for someplace safe to go. We need to find a place to assess his wounds.

As we begin to walk away, I hear the vicious sounds escape the woman again. I look over my shoulder and see her bring herself off the ground. My dad stands there, about six feet from her. I know he's analyzing her every move. With his gun still raised and in proper shooting position, I hear him say, "Please stop. I don't want to hurt you again. Let me help you."

Before he can speak another word to convince her to stop, she leaps at him. There is no stopping the carnage she wishes upon us. The sound of the bullet expelling from the gun surges through my body and echoes through the eerie village. Her body lifelessly hits the ground. My dad does a quick once over of the area surrounding us and turns quickly to catch us. When he catches up, he motions to a barn up ahead.

Skylar is able to temporarily hold Wiley up on her own, so my dad and I can do recon on the barn. We do a complete sweep of the immediate space surrounding the building. The house on the property is far enough away to not be a huge concern. I'm disappointed to see that the door to the barn is shut and the hinge and latch have been weathered together. My dad takes Wiley's arm to steady him, and I ask Skylar to get the flashlight from my backpack. She hands it to me, and I use the blunt bottom to forcefully knock the latch free. The thud is loud, and I hope we haven't drawn any more attention to ourselves, but I keep working on getting the door open. Once the lock finally cracks, Skylar and I quickly open the door far enough to squeeze in as my dad continues to support Wiley. I click the flashlight on and shine the light into the barn. Once the barn is half-ass secured, we all step inside and shut the door as quietly as possible behind us.

CHAPTER SEVEN

MAX: Saturday, May 23

My eyes begin to adjust to the faintly dim interior of the barn. Hanging on the walls on old, rusted metal nails are various old-fashioned farm tools. I recognize old shears, shovels, spades, a few different scythes, knives, and hooks. Bales of straw partially line one wall, and bales of hay line the other side. Everything is outdated but neatly organized.

We help Wiley hobble over to one of the bales and lower him to sit. I toss my backpack on the ground beside him. My dad grabs another bale with ease and places it slightly in front of Wiley to elevate his hurt leg. He whimpers slightly as my dad lifts his leg but catches himself before he makes too much noise.

"Son of a..." he says under his breath as he lets the weight of his leg rest against the bale.

My dad raises Wiley's pant leg and uncovers a somewhat

gaping cut on his shin, just above his ankle. When the woman grabbed his leg, he must have either cut it on something nearby when he went down or maybe her fingernail had dug into his flesh. With a disgusted look, Skylar lets out an "ugh" and turns away to cover her mouth. My dad stands up and looks at Wiley and his leg, as if assessing what needed to be done.

"Okay, we can fix this," he says, perhaps reassuring himself. "We need some water...and a sewing kit." He looks around. "This barn should have that." He then turns his attention to us. "Max, Sky, go look, now."

"Go look over there, I'll cover this side," I say to Skylar.

"Okay," she replies as she walks away, giving me a perplexed look.

At that moment, I'm reminded how her eyes light up her face. A freckle on the crest of her cheekbone reminds me of just how delicate she is. Considering how freaking horrible yesterday was, and the whole camping in the woods overnight thing—she looks as if she's had all the beauty sleep in the world.

Skylar is a natural beauty. Her complexion is flawless, her cheeks maintain their own natural shade of pink, and her long, full eyelashes complement her radiating eyes. Her hair, a mix of honey and whiskey, has been in variations of up and down since our trip started, but not once has it not flattered her picture-perfect face.

Double negative.

Dude, stop staring. She's just a girl. Well, actually she's a woman. Okay, Max, now you're holding a debate with yourself in your head. Cool.

"Hello? Sometime today." My dad probably thinks I'm an idiot at this point.

I shuffle away slightly embarrassed; maybe he just thought I had zoned out. I start making my way around the barn, searching every crevice I can. I find nothing. I look in drawers, under tools, up on the shelves, everywhere. As my search continues, I manage to find a crumpled plastic bottle with what appears to be a few ounces of water inside. I grab it, not knowing if it will be of use or not and make my way back to the others.

Skylar is already with the guys. She hands my dad what she found. I close in and see that she found a travel-size packet of pain reliever. I hold out my slightly empty hands and give him the somewhat empty bottle of water.

I shrug my shoulders. "All I could find."

"I looked everywhere I could. There's nothing but farm tools and pointless knick-knacks."

Skylar chimes in. "Same here, I couldn't find anything either."

"I can go. To that convenience store, I mean. It's not far. I can run there. I'll break in and get what you need. Just a sewing kit and water, right?"

My dad replies, "I really don't think that's the smartest idea. I know I took down that woman, but what if that kid is still out there? Or what if there are others like that. We don't know what we're up against here, Max."

"Well, Dad, it's either I go or you go. One of us has to. We don't have the supplies and it's obvious we need them." I add, "Or would you rather we all go?"

"Okay, okay. I get it," he says, talking with his hands.

"It's probably better for you to stay here anyway and keep an eye on his leg. It should take me like what, ten minutes tops? There and back. Is there anything else you need?"

He thinks for a moment. "A first-aid kit, too, if you can find one. That would help a lot. I know you can do this Max," he says reassuringly. "I can't stress enough that you need to stay alert and watch your back."

Skylar breaks our conversation. "I'm going, too."

The rest of us all reply "no" at the same time. If it weren't for his occasional moans, I would have forgotten about Wiley's presence in the room. He hasn't said much, not even to comment on our supply run, until now. I hope that his cut's not becoming infected. I don't know if whatever is wrong with those people—causing them to lash out and be so violent—is contagious in any way. I fear for him. His face is becoming pale, and he appears to be sweating more than usual.

Skylar reiterates, "I'm going," and then pauses for a slight moment to follow with her defense. "You can't go alone. If I go with you, we can get this done in half the time. I can get one item, and you can get the other. Wham bam, we're back before they even know we left. What if you get in trouble? I'm not completely useless, Max. I'm going."

She did have a point.

And it would be nice to not have to go alone. But I don't want it to be her at risk.

I look at my dad to evaluate his reaction. He looks as if he might actually be considering what she proposed.

"This isn't up for discussion guys, I'm going," she adds as she grabs her gun and throws her backpack over her shoulder. "We'll both take our backpacks in case we find more supplies."

She's at the door before I can object so I tell them, "Be right back."

As I walk away, I give Wiley a reassuring tap on the shoulder. I toss my backpack over my shoulder and meet her at the door.

I pause before opening the door. "When we get out of the barn, we need to wait and check out what's going on. Then, when I give the go ahead, we'll make a run straight for the store. Do you remember where it is?"

She nods to confirm and I continue on. "Do not stop to look

at the flowers, do not collect $200 and pass go, do not get side-tracked in any way. We need to keep focused. Straight there, straight back. We'll figure out who gets what when we get there."

Her face tightens, and I sense her irritation at how I'm treating her right now, but I need her to realize the importance of what we're doing. We can't afford to act foolishly and have another one of us get hurt. We've already had too many close calls, and one of these times, close will be too close.

I open the door and let her walk out ahead of me. She unsteadily raises her gun into position as I walk out behind her. I close the door quietly and begin to do my assessment of our surroundings. A minute goes by, and I feel confident that we're safe to move. I tell her to go ahead and I will follow closely.

"Try to run as quietly as you can. Make sure you keep an eye on the ground, too, to make sure you don't hit anything that will make noise and draw attention to us." She gives me another hurtful look and takes off jogging ahead of me with ease.

We reach the convenience store within two minutes. I approach the front door with caution and stop to look around again. The lights are on in the store, but the black letters on the aged white sign on the front door read "CLOSED."

"Do you see anything?"

She hastily replies, "Don't you think I would have told you if I did?"

"Now isn't the time for attitude, Skylar."

"Oh, really? And when exactly is the time, Max? Maybe treat me like I'm not a complete reject and I won't have such an 'attitude.' Now are you going to break the glass, or am I?"

I try not to let her words bother me too much and continue on with the plan. I pick up one of the paver stones from the poorly put together landscaping and hand it to her, saying, "Be my guest."

The stone breaks through the glass on her first attempt and crashes onto the ground inside the store. The glass continues to crumble onto the ground as I reach my hand through. I fumble around until my hand lands on the lock inside, and I immediately feel like an idiot as I realize the door was already unlocked. I look at Skylar and pull the handle to open the door.

"Was the door seriously unlocked the whole time? Did you not think to check that?"

"Not the time to gloat, Skylar, not the time."

I shake my head in boyish defeat as she grins at me and says, "Honest mistake."

We step over the majority of the glass and close what's left of the door behind us. The store is rather small, with only four aisles.

"Let's make a quick sweep, then we'll get the goods."

I go ahead of her this time and tell her to keep an eye on the door. We make a quick pass through the store to make sure we're secure. I tell her to get the water from the drink section on the far side, and I'll handle getting the sewing kit. There are no signs hanging from the ceiling letting customers know where items are located, but by the size of the store, I don't think it was ever really necessary. I can easily look over each shelf from the standing position and see into each aisle.

Skylar heads to the water, and I make my way into a miscellaneous aisle to try to find a sewing kit. It takes me longer than I'd like to finally locate one but when I find it, I'm pleased that there are many different sized needles and threads. When I look up, I see Skylar's smiling face round the corner with her hands full. I see she's found a large jug of water, a first-aid kit, and snacks.

I smile at her and joke, "What, go on a shopping spree did we?"

She lets out a joyous giggle that sends my heart beating harder and replies, "Well, I got excited, what can I say. I found the water quick and then saw all of this on the way back to you. See this is why I said we both needed our backpacks!"

We take them off and set them on the ground to load them full of all of the stuff we were lucky enough to get. I look up, and a row of sports drinks catches my eye. I grab a few and stuff them into my backpack, too. I can't help but feel an obligation to come back here in the future and repay the owners. I don't want to be a looter, just a survivor. My stomach sinks when my guilt is replaced with sorrow that I may never know the fate of the owners. We finish loading our backpacks, grab our holstered guns, and begin to make our way to the front of the store.

Skylar nudges my arm and says lightly, "See! I told you I could help."

I reply, "Yeah, yeah, but we aren't back yet," and give her a nudge back and a smile.

She winks at me, and I become lost in her. She draws me in. I don't think she even realizes how she entrances me. It's not just her exterior, but her raw interior that I sometimes get to experience. I feel myself lighten when she's around, and I can only hope that she feels that in the slightest.

I hear a movement outside and grab Skylar's arm and nod my head toward the entrance. We stand there perfectly still as we see the little girl that chased us earlier meander across the sidewalk in front of the store. For a moment, I think she'll just pass us by, but then she stops at the mangled front window.

Her behavior changes when she steps on a broken piece of glass. She turns and looks inside the store. A low groan leaves her body—just like the man we hit, the woman by the highway, and the woman in the street earlier. Instinctively, I push Skylar behind me and raise my gun quietly in case the little girl decides to enter the store. I don't want to kill her; I won't kill her; but if she tries to attack us, I'll shoot her so that we can escape.

I don't know what else to do other than wait. I don't want to provoke her, but I also don't want to stand here all day and risk Wiley catching an infection. The little girl just stands there, big-eyed on the other side of the door groaning and grunting.

Skylar whispers, "What should we do?"

I reply, "I guess just wait for her to make a move."

"Are you going to kill her?"

"No," I say immediately, then follow with, "I don't know, I don't want to."

The little girl must have heard us talking because her groans become more rapid and increase in volume. I worry that she may somehow summon other pissed off people to our location.

I whisper to Skylar, "We should throw something past her and try to distract her."

She replies by reaching down and grabbing a can of soup off the shelf and hands it to me. I hand her my gun and take the can of condensed chicken noodle soup. I tiptoe forward just a bit, arch back, and throw the can as precisely as I can. The little girl turns quickly and takes a few steps away from the door to follow the can of soup. Skylar quickly hands me my gun.

Now is our opportunity.

As quietly as I can, I push the door open, and Skylar and I try to sneak our way out. Just as we exit the store, the little girl turns around and locks her eyes on us. She grunts louder than before and starts lurching forward towards us in disturbing motions. I shove Skylar and tell her to run. She takes off running and I follow her. Only a few strides in, a large man appears from an alley nearly ten feet away, stopping us dead in our tracks. The groans escaping him are the same as the little girls.

We are trapped between a very angry small child, and a very angry large man.

I turn so my back is to Skylar as we circle around in our confinement.

CHAPTER EIGHT

MAX: Saturday, May 23

She frantically mutters, "Max, WHAT do we do?"

I reply back with the only thing that comes to mind: "Shoot."

As soon as the word evaporates into the air, both the girl and man leap at us with viciousness gleaming across their faces. They want nothing else but to hurt us.

I feel the movement of Skylar drawing her gun at the same time I do. As soon as we are in position, we have no choice but to shoot. I fire once, hitting my target immediately and Skylar shoots twice to make her impact on the man. One small thud followed by one large thud as their lifeless bodies hit the ground.

I drop to my knees; I've won but I am defeated.

I put my head in my hands in utter disbelief that I just shot, and killed a child—a small, helpless little girl that will never get to know her adolescence. I killed her.

The recoil of the gun lingers on my wrist, and the smell of gunpowder fills my lungs. I kneel as the world spins for what feels like forever but is probably only less than a minute. Skylar puts her arms around me from behind and holds me tight. She says quietly, "It could have been anyone. You had to do it, Max. It was them, or us. You made the right decision."

She's right, but it doesn't make what I just did any easier to swallow. I begin to feel sick to my stomach.

I stand up, holding onto the grip she has around my waist and with my back still to her, tell her, "Don't tell them what I've done."

She replies calmly, "Okay." I let go of her grip, and her hands stay around my waist for a slight moment before falling to the side.

It hits me how selfish I am in this moment.

"Are you okay?" I ask her.

"I don't want to talk about it," she replies. I can hear the internal pain she's trying to disguise.

"Okay...let's go," I urge.

And before we can talk about anything else and waste any more valuable time, we're off. We run straight back to the barn. Upon arrival, we do a quick check to make sure that we haven't been followed and are safe to enter. When I open the door, my dad is standing immediately on the other side with a sickened look on his face.

Urgency lines his voice. "What happened? Is everything okay? I heard gunshots, I was just about to leave to come after you."

Skylar quickly responds to his questions, "Yeah we're fine. We came into contact with a large male showing signs of the same behavior and we were forced to take him down."

She pauses and then starts again. "I was able to find all of the supplies you wanted and even extra stuff to keep us going. How's my uncle?"

She starts unloading her backpack near Wiley. My dad, who seems to accept the response, follows her over to see what we brought back. I shut the barn door behind me all of the way and stand there for a moment. I look over, and Skylar motions and says, "I think the first-aid kit is in your backpack. Can I have one of those Gatorades?"

I hand Skylar my backpack. She fishes out the supplies to tend to Wiley's wound and hands them to Dad. While we were gone my dad was able to get Wiley to choke down the travel pack of Advil and rig up a little area to try to make him more comfortable. He moves quickly as he begins meticulously cleaning Wiley's wound with some of the water from the jug. Wiley winces and groans slightly. From the grip he holds on the bale, I can only assume he is in quite a bit of pain. After a few minutes pass of cleaning the cut, my dad says, "Good news, I don't think it's infected. Minimal swelling and redness, but we need to get it stitched up as soon as possible."

Wiley weakly replies, "The sooner the better. I can't handle much more poking and prodding."

"You're doing really good, bud."

Unwrapping the packaging on the sewing kit my dad says, "This is great. I was hoping there would be multiple needles to choose from."

"I'm going to keep a watch by the door...just in case," I say. Personally, I didn't want to sit there and watch a needle and string go in and out of someone's leg. With everything that keeps happening, I need a moment, partially, to myself anyway.

I don't wait for approval, I just go ahead and walk to the barn door. I decide to pull a nearby bale of hay over to sit on while I keep watch. I wrap my fingers under the twine and hoist it to an appropriate spot. I sit there for a few more moments, staring blankly at the floor. I try not to think of anything. It's like I'm giving my mind a break, to just be free for a while. I'm not sure how much time has passed when Skylar walks up and my concentration on nothing is broken. She holds out a bottle of Gatorade and a protein bar.

I say, "Thank you," softly and accept them.

She half smiles and turns to walk back to the guys. I appreciate the caring distance she gives me. I hadn't realized how fatigued I'd become until I start on the Gatorade. I finish the bottle in almost one chug.

I look over to check the progress my dad is making with Wiley. He's just completed the stitching and is adding the finishing touches of wrapping the wound. I take this opportunity to walk back over and ask, "So, what's the plan now?"

My dad replies without taking his eyes away from his task. "Well, I think it's only fair to let Wiley rest a little bit, at least a couple hours. And I think it would be good for all of us to take a short break, too. The barn has proven to be fairly secure, so I think we should all rest for a little bit and then go back at it. If we don't let Wiley rest now, we won't be moving any faster."

"Okay, that's fine. I'm going to set up another bale by the door and lie down up there. I should be able to hear well from there."

"Have either of you two checked your phones?"

"Yeah, nothing. I mean it works, and it says there's a signal, but the little circle dude keeps spinning and nothing happens."

"Mine, too," Skylar adds.

"Server overload, probably."

As I go to walk away, Skylar catches my arm. "I can stay up there with you if you want to doze off," she suggests. "I'll stay awake if you need a break."

"I'm fine. I don't need to sleep. Stay back here with your

uncle; he may need you. You should try to get some rest, your-self, too."

I turn to walk away and see the disappointment spread across her face. I quickly add, "But thank you though. I'll let you know if I need the break."

A piece of hay pokes me in the face, and I quickly realize that I've fallen asleep. I look down at my watch and see that it's 2:10 p.m. We've stayed here longer than we should have. I stand up to stretch and see that everyone else is fast asleep, too. In any other situation, or world, I would lie back down and let everyone sleep. Well, in any other situation we wouldn't be taking naps in barns. Today is different, though. We can't risk being out here any longer.

I walk over and nudge my dad's foot to wake him up. He jumps up, startled. He quickly realizes it's me, and his demeanor changes. He stretches his arms and then looks down at his watch.

"Shit," he says. "Wake Sky. I'll wake Wiley and check his ankle."

I walk over to where she's lying and kneel down beside her. I'm cautious not to wake her just yet. For a moment, I just admire her. With all the unknown brutality surrounding us, I've found an angel among all these demons. She looks so peaceful while she sleeps, like a child, who you know could easily terrorize your life when they wake. I place my hand on her shoulder and give her a faint nudge to wake her up. I watch as her eyes flutter open and tell her, "It's time to wake up. We need to get going."

She moves to a sitting position and rubs her eyes sleepily.

We stand up and walk over to Wiley and my dad. Wiley

has already awoken, and he and my dad are discussing his level of pain.

"I actually feel pretty good, considering." He extends an arm. "Here, help me up."

My dad helps him stand, and he insists on walking around to test his ankle. When he takes his first step, he stumbles slightly but immediately regains balance and is able to carefully walk around without help. After a couple of laps around the barn, he's easily walking at a much more normal pace.

"I really don't feel much pain anymore. It's just more," he pauses for a second, "sore than hurt." He extends his hand to my dad. "Thank you, Keith."

Dad grabs Wiley's hand in his and gives it a firm shake. "Hey buddy, you woulda done the same for me. Glad to see you're feeling better."

He turns to us. "Alright gang, we need to get a move on it. No knowing what's developed out there. The building we're going to shouldn't be more than a quick walk through the field to the southeast. Let's grab our stuff and head out."

A few murmured "okays" and we're off to start packing our things into our backpacks.

We make our way to the barn door and stop to quickly devise a plan. We stay quiet for a few minutes to make sure nothing is close by and then slowly open the barn door. When we're all out of the barn, I slowly shut the door behind us. We begin walking what must be southeast according to my dad's prior declaration. Jogging would be much more desirable at this point, but with Wiley's condition, jogging will be reserved for emergency situations only.

As we make our way a little farther, we pass the house that belongs to the barn. I see no sign of occupancy. As we pass the farthest side of the house something catches my eye spewed out in big, red, painted letters across the porch: *PRAY FOR OUR NATION*.

"Look," I say. They all turn around to read the haunting words. In our day and age, it's hard to know the mindset of the typical American, so deciding whether these letters were written in the past or present is difficult to determine, although, I'm leaning towards the latter.

Eagerness sinks in every time we get in eyesight range of any buildings. I keep thinking we're reaching our next rendezvous point, but my dad assures me we haven't. Every building we pass has looked exactly the same, so I'm not sure how my dad knows which one we're actually looking for. I look ahead and my eyes fixate on three buildings in the distance. They're close together—one of the buildings is rather large with two smaller shed-sized buildings nearby. My dad nudges my arm and smirks as he nods forward. We have arrived.

We've been walking along the tree line in order to not expose ourselves, if anyone happens to be around, although there was not a car in sight on either of the side streets we darted across. We duck inside the trees and stop for a minute to make sure we're alone and come to the conclusion that we're the only ones out in the middle of this nowhere.

One by one we cover each other and make our way to the biggest of the three buildings. It appears to be just one of those buildings that farmers use to store their equipment. Doubt begins to form as I think that my dad has walked us almost an hour out of our way for nothing. We reach the door to the building, and my doubts are erased when I see that it has a complicated key code entry attached. I've been around enough farming in my life to determine this isn't typical.

Almost immediately, my dad starts meticulously pushing sequences of buttons on the entry pad. Skylar stays with my dad—doing what I think she thinks is guarding him—as Wiley and I venture around the building. She looks more like a confused, lost puppy. Everything about the way she holds a gun is unnatural and makes me aware that she is not the same girl proficiently holding a loaded weapon to my chest.

She is not the same girl that I sometimes fear from my dream.

We take the opportunity to venture around the other two small buildings. Farm equipment peeks out from under the tarps and makes me feel unsettled about my dad's desire to come here. I'm about to head back when I see a tan fender protruding from underneath a tarp. Wiley catches my curiosity and follows me to an open overhang of the building. As quietly as possible, Wiley helps me uncover our hidden treasure. This extra stop completely pays off when I see what's hiding under this tarp.

The side-badge states "MRZR 4" and the imprint on the front, above the grill says "POLARIS." I turn to Wiley, who looks completely un-phased by our fortune, and say, "We just hit the jackpot." I've played enough PS4 to recognize this military-grade off-road combat vehicle.

"But how do we start it?" he adds.

I guess with all of my excitement I forgot the most obvious fact that we don't know where the key to this bad boy is. I jump inside and motion for Wiley to come closer as I start to fumble with the instrument panel inside of our new UTV. I think back to when I was a child, out at the cabin, watching my dad hot-wire an old truck. The ignition had locked up on us while out cruising around our thirty acres. I hope, to myself, that the steps are somewhat the same for this vehicle.

I haven't made much progress when out of the corner of my eye I see Skylar waving her arm to notify us to come back. We jump out and begin to jog back to the biggest of the buildings. Midway I tell Wiley I'll catch up to him and turn around to head back to the UTV. I decide to throw the tarp back over the unit, just in case someone were to drive by.

There is an access road that the building is exposed to—not that people are out for a weekend cruise, but you never know. I just don't want anyone to know of our presence here, especially while we have no game plan for getting this thing started. I'm sure my dad should be able to start it. I've never actually hotwired anything before, and even though I know the general steps to take, I'll probably screw something up if I do it myself.

When I reach the others, my dad informs me that he cracked their security, and as soon as he pushes the last sequence, the door will unlock. For a split second, I'm reminded that my dad knows entirely more than I thought he did. I push it back in the "figure dad out" file and save it for another day.

Together we draw our weapons proactively as he keys in the last few buttons to open the door. None of us make a sound as we hear the click of the electric lock. We hear a series of deadbolt locks turning themselves to the unlocked position. With his free hand, my dad reaches for the doorknob.

He turns to me and nods. "Let's do this."

CHAPTER NINE

MAX: Saturday, May 23

My dad opens the door slowly and steps inside. We use solid, cautious movements as we follow his lead. He pauses for a moment, and I hear Skylar's staggered breathing behind me. In this moment, I remember that she is still just a young, terrified girl, trying her best to conform to the new reality we've all been thrown into.

Our world has been torn to shambles. We've spent the last twenty-four hours running from a decently organized group of people who we aren't even sure who they are, except that they are powerful enough to have overthrown our society. Not to mention, she's probably super thrilled about almost being murdered a few times by crazy people.

My thoughts head back to reality when my dad flips the light switch on and the door clicks shut behind Skylar. In the middle of the room is a large black crate, and at the back of the room, there are various shelves with totes and smaller crates. I follow my dad's gaze back to the panel with the light switch. On the side, furthest away from the door, hang two keys on golden hooks. As he goes to grab them, he stops dead in his tracks at the gravel crunching, signifying a vehicle arriving outside of the building.

"Quick, behind the shelves! Quiet!" he says in a hushed but urgent manner as he flicks the lights off and follows swiftly after us, pushing us on his way.

I feel my blood start to boil and my cheeks flush as I realize if someone enters those doors, we're stuck, trapped in this building with no way out. Wiley goes behind the shelves first, followed by Skylar, myself, then my dad. We kneel down, draw our guns in suspense of what is about to unfold.

The sound of the electronic buttons on the door fills the space around us. My heart sinks. I feel sick to my stomach as I bite the inside of my lip to resist making a sound. I don't breathe; I can't breathe, but I hear Skylar's breathing become more erratic, so I nudge her and tell her as quietly as possible, "Shh." She leans into me, and I start to worry that she might pass out.

I hear the sound of the deadbolts unlocking—the same sound I was so freaking happy to hear just a few minutes ago. A similar panic to what I felt when I saw that guard grab Skylar by the throat hits me.

The door opens. I blink a few times to help my eyes adjust, and the light from outside is enough to give me a clear view of a man as he walks through the entrance and stops. I look between the roughly half-inch gap between crates at him. I feel the pressure of Skylar's body press further into my side, and I let the weight of her fall against me without resisting. With my free hand, I reach across my lap and reassuringly rest my hand on her knee.

I don't know what I'm trying to assure her, that she won't

die alone? She gently, and almost silently, places her soft, small hand on top of mine. Maybe she's reassuring me of the same thing.

After a few moments, I hear the man's voice loudly call, "All clear! Sanchez will be here at fifteen hundred for the crate contents and UTV. Clear out!" Skylar's hand tightens its grip around mine. We continue to sit like statues as we hear the man, and the few others make their way back to their vehicles. An engine starts, and I hear dirt speckle the building as they quickly drive away. I click the button on my watch that illuminates the background. 2:55pm.

We have five minutes.

My dad breaks the silence by saying, "Come on." He stands up and pulls at my arm, releasing the bittersweet embrace Skylar and I had. We rush back to the middle of the room.

"Wait here, I'll flip the switch."

I reply, "Dad, shouldn't we just leave? The other group will be here in less than five minutes. Are we really going to risk getting caught?"

I know there is no changing his mind when he doesn't even respond. I hear him rush to the door and turn the lights on.

My eyes adjust themselves once again as I locate the crate. I feel Skylar's presence at my elbow, and I turn around and give her a grim smile. It's all I can muster in this moment, and I assume the same for her when I receive the same one back.

My dad arrives with both keys. He tries the first one in the lock. No success. He shoves that key into his pocket; I wonder why he even keeps it, as its purpose seems quite useless at this point. He places the next key strategically into the lock on the crate, and I feel such a relief when I see his hand turn it successfully. I have no idea what is in this crate, but if some military man named Sanchez is coming to get it, I want first dibs.

His face reads both excitement and anxiety as he quickly begins to remove the lock. He seems rather pleased with himself that he was able to break in. When he lifts the top, we give each other satisfied, smug looks. Oh, how incredibly convenient that everything in this box is in a multiple of four. Tucked tightly and cleanly inside this crate are four handguns with an extra extended magazine each, eight boxes of ammunition, and four small Tasers. I'm not disappointed, but I thought there may have been something else in here.

My dad grabs my backpack and tosses it at me. "Backpacks. Load one set of each in your backpack. Hurry!"

We do as he says and shove one set of each into our backpacks. He carefully shuts the crate and places the key back on the golden hook where he pulled it from just moments ago. I briefly fill my dad in on the UTV that Wiley and I found. He taps his pocket and smirks. "I've got the key in my pocket." Of course he does.

I feel so stupid for thinking that he should have thrown that key to the ground. I'm more relieved that we won't have to hotwire it and risk damaging anything, though. There is still silence from outside, but it's only a few more minutes before Sanchez and whoever else is due to arrive, so we have to act as quickly as possible. We don't know him or his intentions, but if I were him, I'd be pissed we just stole his shit.

My dad slowly turns the door handle and gently and cautiously opens the door. We continue to hear silence outside so he uses his gun to open the door further and take a look. The UTV is around a hundred feet away. Skylar and Wiley are the slowest so we tell them to go first. My dad and I cover them and then take off behind them in a staggered manner.

So far, so good.

We all arrive at the UTV at the same time, and Wiley and I quickly rip the tarp off and throw it to the ground. I'm pleased that it's the crew cab edition so there are seats for all four of us. There is also an open storage area in the back where two people could actually ride if necessary. It even has the means to mount a .50 cal to the back of it. This thing is badass.

Wiley and my dad hop in the two front seats, Skylar and I in the back. My dad puts the key into the ignition and turns the engine over. Nothing. No response. *Shit.* I quickly realize, I had pulled a few wires when I was trying to figure out how to hot-wire it.

"Dad, down low, the wires. Re-attach them," I say with regret and urgency in my voice.

As he begins to fumble with the wires, I look up and see two men walking around the building. Since Wiley is already in a crouched position trying to help my dad, I quickly grab Skylar and push her downward. I whisper to them all: "Up ahead. Two men thirty feet away."

Speeding up his pace, Dad continues to mess with the wires. I begin to get that sickening panic sweeping throughout my body, again. We're down far enough to where we should be out of sight, but the tarp is lying on the ground, completely exposing the UTV.

I hear my dad cheerfully whisper, "Got it!" as he reaches up to turn the key over in the ignition. The engine of the UTV comes to life, and I feel a tinge of hope course through my body, pushing away the intense panic that had been creeping in.

We lift our heads as my dad pushes on the accelerator, and I see the man who was about thirty feet away, now at about ten feet and closing. As we whiz by, I catch the look on his face: angry, but also hopeless. Every ounce of hope I just gained had just been robbed of this man.

I look to his side and see that he is carrying a weapon, and I can't help but be confused as to why he chose not to draw it on us. He doesn't shoot, he doesn't scream, he just simply puts his hands forward as to suggest for us to stop. Of course, we don't. I feel the slightest bit of guilt for stealing these men's precious weapons and vehicle, but then I hastily remember the world we now live in. We have to do what's best for us.

I still feel uneasy, but for a change I feel a sense of safety. We have more protection, and now, transportation. And we still have each other. I look to my left and give Skylar a reassuring smile, but instead, this time there is more emotion behind it. She reaches over and places her hand on my knee and gives it a slight squeeze, returning the assuring gesture.

We move east at a relatively fast pace. Our terrain is sporadic. One minute we're moving along very smoothly, and then the next we hit turbulence. Although the suspension of this UTV is very solid and versatile and takes the majority of the impact successfully, I still brace myself tightly in case we hit something too abruptly.

We approach an area that is completely flat but covered in trees and shrubs. The landscape is breathtaking. Weeds have grown up, and wildflowers are all around. I daydream for a moment that life is back to normal, and we're just cruising through the woods, enjoying this beautiful day.

The ground is covered in purple wildflowers. My mother's favorite color was purple, and at our cabin she had a massive garden full of different types of purple flowers—clematis, lavender, sage, hydrangea. It's moments like this I'm reminded of how much I miss her.

Sometimes it doesn't seem so long ago that she was here—walking me to school and baking me cookies. That woman knew her way in and out of almost any situation. It'll be six years this fall, and it never seems to get any easier; the pain just becomes dull.

My memory of her and the purple flowers is tainted when I hear my dad say, "Ugh, guys, we may have a problem."

I lean forward. "What kind of problem?"

"Well, I hadn't checked since we left in such a hurry, but, um...it appears we're about to run out of fuel."

"Are you kidding me?"

Skylar chimes in. "We can stop and siphon some, right? What kind of fuel does this take anyways?"

My dad replies, "Yeah, that's a great idea, but look around us. Nothing but trees and fields. I think there is a set of railroad tracks soon though, so we could probably follow it until the next station and hopefully get some fuel." He pauses and then starts in again. "But that's if we make it that far. We're running really low, and I've already switched over to the reserve fuel."

Just as he finishes speaking, the UTV starts sputtering.

"I think we should just park over there." I point ahead at the tree line. "We can try to camouflage this thing and then go ahead on foot to the railroad tracks. We can walk until we find fuel and bring it back."

"How will we bring it back?" Skylar asks.

"Gatorade bottles," I say, matter-of-factly.

Wiley says, "I'm feeling a lot better now, so don't disagree with his plan because of me. I think it's the best idea so far."

Skylar says half sarcastically, "Well, it's the only idea so far."

I reply hastily, "Okay, Einstein, do you have another idea?"

"No, I was just stating a fact, don't get so uptight."

My dad cuts us off. "Really guys? Right now is when you choose to bicker? Cut it out."

I reply, "Whatever." We hit a bump and my speech is interrupted. "What do you want to do?"

"Another option would be to run this thing completely out of fuel, but that seems to be approaching rather quickly. Or we could split up—half of us getting fuel, the other half staying here."

I dislike both of his ideas. "Yeah, I'm not liking either one of those ideas. I think we need to stay together. We don't know what we're up against out here," I say as I point to the field of nothing but trees all around us. We really don't know who, or what could be lurking behind those trees.

I also dislike the fact that if we split into two groups, I'll either be with Skylar, or without her, and I'm not sure I want to do either right now. Her presence is both an irritation, and necessity. My dad is right, Skylar and I do bicker, a lot, but it's honestly what's keeping me going right now. Without her, I may have broken down by now. In a way, she keeps me on my toes, but keeps me strong. I feel the need to put up a front around her, to be strong and hopeful so she doesn't fear.

There is a robust group of trees ahead that we decide to pull into before we completely run out of fuel. We jump out and gather our belongings. After piling up our stuff nearby, we begin grabbing twigs and branches from the nearby trees to use as camouflage.

My dad and I are better at strategically placing the branches to maximize their usefulness, so Skylar and Wiley spend their time gathering and bringing them to us. I hear Skylar struggling and turn to see her carrying a foliage-covered branch twice her size. I jump from the fender of the UTV and jog over to her.

"Wow, good job. This one will be super helpful. Here, let me take it."

She cuts me off and breathily says, "I can carry it. Just let me do it."

"I didn't mean anything by it, Skylar, I just thought I could help."

"I'm fine, I'll carry it to you. You can go back," she says as she struggles to move the branch a few feet.

"Well, I'll at least help you. I'm already here. Let me grab this end, you can carry that end. We really don't need to argue about this—I know you're capable of carrying it."

She stops for a second and stares at me. Her eyes are piercing, and I have to swallow the lump that's formed in my throat. I brace for whatever reaction she's about to give me.

She shifts the weight of the branch. "Fine, grab this end, I'll get this end."

She probably rolled her eyes in the process, but at least she's willing to let me help. I didn't mean to make her feel inferior: she honestly looked like she was struggling and needed help. Plus, we *are* kind of on a time schedule here.

We carry the branch the final distance to the UTV, and I ask for her help lifting it onto the roof. I try to make it clear that I don't think she's completely useless. We hoist the branch far enough for my dad to grab. I jump from the fender to the roof with a swift motion and finish helping him pull it on top. The branches are so leaf-covered that nearly the whole top of the UTV and hood are covered.

While we finish securing the rest of the branches around the side, I remember that I shoved my portable GPS in my backpack when we were at our house. I hop down and start rummaging through my backpack and say to Skylar, "Hey, grab your journal, I need you to write something down."

She gives me a puzzled look but reaches into her backpack and pulls out her journal. I power up the GPS and read her the coordinates to our exact location.

I jokingly say, "Never know how well our camo will work. We may forget where we were."

We walk east towards the railroad tracks and follow the same formation we typically do: my dad in front, Wiley and Skylar side by side in the middle, and me, following up in the rear. We walk for a while in silence. A person could almost assume we were the last people on earth. The only sounds are those of nature around us and the crumpling of dirt and leaves beneath our feet.

I'm listening intently to the sound of two birds chattering back and forth to each other when I hear a sharp whistle. I look behind us, and in the distance, a train is approaching. By now, the rest of the group has caught on to the new sound. My dad speaks up and says, "The train appears to be moving backward. The conductor's box is probably on the opposite end of what we're seeing."

Skylar says inquisitively, "So, if I'm not mistaken, we should be able to hop aboard this train, and ride it until we find fuel without anyone potentially seeing us?"

"Well, it's a good theory," he replies. "The train doesn't appear to be moving too fast, so we should all be able to hop on with ease. If it stays at a consistent speed like this, we should be able to safely hop off of it, too."

I chime in, "I'm game. Wiley, how are you feeling about this?"

CHAPTER TEN

MAX: Saturday, May 23

"Hey, I'm always game to do life-threatening shit," he says sarcastically. "Seriously though, that idea sounds better than walking right now." He adds, "Plus, we'll be able to see around us and choose the best place to fuel up."

"Alright, well, we've got a few minutes before it's close enough to hop on. Make sure all of your stuff is secure. Let's get our game faces on. Max, you and I will head towards the train and get on first. We'll be able to help Wiley and Skylar get on as we pass them."

He's talking with his hands again.

"I'll help Wiley, you can help Skylar...unless you're feeling stronger than your ol' man today?" He nudges me and cracks a smile.

"I'll let you show off for once, okay?" I say as I nudge him back with an amused look.

He looks at the rest of the group. "Sound like a plan?"

They both shake their head in agreement.

My dad and I start walking towards the train, and just as we get out of earshot, he asks me, "Now you're not afraid you'll catch cooties from Skylar, are you? You two act like each other has the plague sometimes."

I look at him and roll my eyes. "Cooties, really, Dad?"

"Well, I'm not blind, deaf, or stupid. One minute you two are flirting, and the next I feel like I should take the guns away from both of you." I don't respond, and his sarcastic demeanor shifts to serious. "One thing is for sure though, you both feel strongly for each other; I just don't know yet if it's in a positive or negative way."

I didn't realize how blatantly obvious whatever is going on with us was until my dad put it this way. I don't know what we are. Part of me wants to run as far away from her as I can, and part of me never wants to leave her side.

I pause for a second and respond as honestly as I can. "I don't know either, Dad."

Our conversation is brought to an end as we near the approaching train. We pick up our pace to a light jog. To our advantage, the boxcar is empty with doors wide open. My dad, who is running a bit faster ahead of me, grabs onto the handle on the side of the train and hoists himself aboard with little effort. I follow his lead and with the same motions, I pull myself on board next to him. I'm a little less graceful than he, so it takes me a split second to regain my balance.

He grabs my arm to help me stabilize and says, "Get ready, we're almost to Sky and Wiley."

Through the wide-open door, I can see them as we approach. They're a little spaced out with Wiley closest to us. My dad jogs to the furthest opening from me, and as he climbs partially out, he grabs onto one of the handles just outside of the boxcar. He holds on with his left arm and leaves his right arm dangling for Wiley to grab onto.

He yells, "Get into position!"

I nod and rush to the furthest opening away from him.

I grab onto the handle and let myself partially hang outside of the train. The feelings coursing through my body are both exhilarating and refreshing. I've never ridden a train before, let alone hung out of one while it's moving. My newfound adrenaline rush is replaced by panic as I feel the train suddenly pick up speed. My body jolts, and I turn to my dad.

He shouts, "Don't think about it. Just do what you're supposed to do. Get her on this train." His voice is stern and solid.

We close in on Wiley as he jogs towards the train. His face shows fear and doubt as he reaches his arms forward to latch onto my dad's free arm. I lock my eyes onto Skylar about one hundred feet away, jogging towards us as the train closes the space between. I hear Wiley let out a groan when his body thrusts against the door of the boxcar. I assume he made it safely when I hear him thank my dad, but I don't dare take my eyes off of Skylar.

I begin to think for a moment that the conductor is aware of our presence when the train begins to gain speed yet again. Perhaps he is trying to disallow us from boarding. I crouch down and extend my free arm. Just before the train is about to pass her, she jumps forward and grabs onto my arm. Instinctively and immediately, I pull her off the ground onto the small step outside of the train. The footing is so small that we're forced to share the tiny amount of space.

The train accelerates and jolts us forward. As fear washes across her face, Skylar loses her footing and falls. Her feet dangle across the ground as I try to maintain my hold of her arms.

In absolute terror she calls out, "Don't let me fall!"

She hasn't taken her grip off of my arm since she first grabbed onto me. Her feet dangle against the ground and she continues to slip away from me. I clutch onto her arms tighter and pull with everything I have. I pull her so forcefully that she takes a solid impact as she crashes against the side of the boxcar. She loses grip on my arm, and just as she is about to fall again, I'm forced to grab her around the waist and pull her against me.

I hold onto her and refuse to let her go.

I tighten my grip around her waist and pull her closer. Her head is positioned on my chest right below my chin. She frees her right arm from between us and reaches around my side to hold onto me. Despite the speed of the train and all of the other movements, I feel her body tremble in my grip.

I whisper to her, "I wasn't going to let you fall, I promise."

She raises her head from my chest to look up at me, possibly considering the words I've just spoken. She looks frightened, and my stomach sinks as I realize I've almost failed her. I don't want her to fear. I want to be the one thing she can truly count on. I will protect her. I will do everything I can to not let her down.

I feel a hand grab onto my shoulder and am brought back to reality when my dad and Wiley pull Skylar and me into the train car. Wiley looks at me intently and says, "Thank you, Max...for saving her. Wholeheartedly, I can't thank you enough."

I reply back, "I'll do everything I can to make sure nothing like that happens again. I'm sorry I let it happen." I turn to look at Skylar and see that she's standing on the inside of the boxcar right where I almost lost her.

I shake Wiley's hand and he gives me a half hug.

He starts to say, "Max, it wasn't your fau—" but I interrupt him and say, "Give me a minute," and turn to walk away. I walk over to her and place my hand on her shoulder. She doesn't turn around, but her body tenses.

"Are you okay?"

She replies in almost a cracked whisper, "No."

"Talk to me," I say to her, concerned.

"I'm...scared."

"I meant what I said, Skylar. I will do everything I can to protect you."

She leans into the hand that I still have rested on her shoulder. I take this cue to step forward, and as I do, she turns around and wraps her arms around my waist. I grab onto the railing to brace us and use my other arm to secure her against me. Her once perfect hair is beginning to tangle, and the impact from the side of the train has already left a bruised and bloody mark across her face. I hate myself for letting this happen.

I whisper to her, "I promise."

She looks up at me, and with defeat in her eyes she says, "What if it's not enough?"

I don't know what to say. Every fiber in my being wants to reassure her that I will protect her, but have I given her reason to believe me? I don't say anything, I just tighten the grasp I have around her body and hold her tighter. I need to get my mind back to more pressing matters, but all I want to do is make her feel safe. I need to make her feel safe.

I hear my dad say loudly to Wiley, "Have you seen anything?" and I assume he's trying to get my attention, too. I turn my head and see that he's looking at me. Without letting go of her, I say to him, "What's the plan?"

He responds loudly, "Well we've gone a few miles at this speed. I feel like now we're starting to slow. I think we should find a good point to hop back off, if we get to a safe enough speed. No taking risks like we just did again. Next time we all jump at once."

I feel Skylar tense against my chest. I nod to my dad in agreement, and I whisper again to Skylar, "I promise."

Our bodies are so close that they're practically fused together. I don't want to let her go, but I need to talk to my dad about the plan. I begin to move us away from the entrance and to a safer spot inside the boxcar.

I tell her softly, "Hang out here for a minute while I go talk to the guys. Okay?"

She agrees and sits down in the corner against the wall. I hold her hand for stability as she sits down. "I'll be right back," I say.

I walk to the opposite side to where Wiley and my dad are standing. Before I can get a word out, Dad asks, "How is she doing?"

"I think she's just a little freaked out. We've had too many close calls. I wouldn't be surprised if she got a concussion when I pulled her back up."

"I'll check her out, but the lighting in here isn't great. May have to wait until we're off the train." He points to Wiley and says, "He took a pretty big hit too, but his skull must be harder than hers. You doing okay, Wiley?"

"Yeah," he says with a pained smile, "I'm fine."

I know he's not fine—between the laceration to his leg, and the hit to the head—but I know he doesn't want to be the one to slow us down anymore.

"What about you buddy, you okay?" Dad asks me.

I nod and ask my dad, "And what about you?"

"Nothing I can't handle." He pauses and tries to change the conversation. He says hesitantly and more seriously, "Max, I'm glad you two seem to be getting along right now, and I know she needs you to be strong for her, but don't let your judgments get clouded. Remember the plan."

"I was just making sure she was okay, and helping her sit

down, that's it. There's nothing else. Now on to more important things, have you guys come up with a plan yet?" I'm lying through my teeth, and I wonder if they buy it.

While we're talking, the train's speed has been steadily decreasing, and we decide this is our opportunity to depart safely.

My dad urges, "Get her now."

I run back over to the other side of the train car. "Skylar, we've got to go, now. The train's slow enough that we need to jump." I grab her hand and pull her to her feet. She looks fearful, so I try to reassure her. "It'll be easier this time. I'm going to help you. C'mon."

We grab our backpacks as the train continues to slow down. I holler to my dad, "Let's help them off first, and then you and I can jump behind them."

My dad and I get Skylar and Wiley into position. We're back to the small foothold that caused so many issues earlier. I have her hold onto the railing on the outside and step onto the outside step.

"We're barely moving; you can do this. Now I'm going to count to three, and on three I want you to jump. I'll be right behind you, I promise."

She looks up at me with her pained eyes and says, "Okay."

"One...Two..." The train begins to accelerate. Before I can allow her to process what is happening, I shout, "Three!" and she and Wiley both jump. I see them both tumble to the ground and immediately get back up. They both shake the dirt off of themselves, seemingly fine.

I shout across to my dad, "It's now or never!"

The train jolts forward as it accelerates. We look at each other, shout "Now!" and jump at the same time. The impact of the ground hits me dead on my side, knocking the wind from my lungs for second and turning my vision black. The sharp and full pain on my side is intense. I'm not sure if I'm seriously injured, but at least I'm slowly regaining my vision. The pain begins to subside slightly and then maintains a dull throb.

Approaching, my dad says, "Max, are you okay? Why aren't you moving?"

He's standing above me, dusting himself off. Behind him I see Skylar in a panic as she's running towards me.

She reaches me and places her hands under my arms to help me get off the ground.

"Oh my God, Max, are you okay? You hit the ground so hard. Is it your head? Or your arm?"

I interrupt her. "No, it's my side. Knocked the damn wind out of myself. It's okay though, I'm fine. Let's go."

I dust myself off lazily with my right arm and notice that I'm subconsciously holding my left arm to my left side. I motion for the rest of the group to come on and begin to walk away. As I take my first step, a sharp pain shoots through my torso and doubles me over. Skylar grabs my arm to help stabilize me.

"I'm fine, really, let's go," I say stubbornly.

I stand up as straight as possible and take another tentative step. The fiery pain shoots through my body, and I wince as I force myself to not go down again. With each step, I trick my mind to forget the bursts of hot pain.

My dad suggests that I stay in the middle and he and Wiley would lead and tail the group. I insist that I'm fine and take my normal formation in the back. Part of me does this so they can't see the struggle I have with each step. I try not to gasp as I talk but breathing deeply causes fierce pain to strike through my body.

My dad turns around to say, "Tree line up ahead. Let's head there and appraise our damage. Sky, I still need to check out the cut on your face."

I feel a tinge of guilt as I remember the bloody injury I caused Skylar.

She replies, "My face is fine. It stopped bleeding, just sore now. I'm more worried about whatever Max is hiding under his shirt."

Apparently, I'm not doing a good job of hiding my pain. I don't say anything, partially because I know they won't believe me, and partially because it hurts to speak.

We reach a safe spot within the trees and set up a temporary camp quickly. The last few cars of the train speed by as we watch from a safe, somewhat-secure distance. I hobble over to Skylar to check her face. I struggle to lift my hand and place it gently along her cheek. She winces as I touch her. The skin around her cheek has turned a prominent shade of scarlet and is swollen. At the base of her cheekbone, a bloodstained laceration has just stopped bleeding. I look into her eyes. The pain I feel that I allowed her to get hurt is greater than the pain I feel in my side.

I let my arm fall back to my side and gently say again, "I'm sorry."

"It wasn't your fault. And it's not up for discussion. Now, raise your shirt. Let your dad look at whatever you're hiding."

My dad approaches. "Sky, I'll have a look at your face in just a minute. Max, what's going on under there?"

I try to shake them off and refuse to let them look, but every move makes me wince with pain. Skylar reaches forward and grabs onto my left arm. Before I can react, she raises it quickly but gently and takes hold of the base of my shirt. I'm forced to bite the inside of my lip to stop myself from wincing or making a noise. As Skylar raises my shirt, she gasps and my dad becomes more alert in his examination.

"What?"

"Buddy, you've got quite a few bruised ribs. I wouldn't be

surprised if a few of them are fractured. What on earth did you hit when you landed?"

"The earth," I say sarcastically. And as I slightly chuckle, pain soars through my side.

"Can you take a deep breath?"

"I don't want to try."

"Okay so I'll take that as a no." My dad ponders for a second. "I hate to say it, but there's really not much we can do for this. We've got mild pain pills in the first-aid kit but that's about it."

My dad walks away to get the first-aid kit. Skylar takes her hand off of my arm and places her palm against my rib cage, as gently as I placed my hand on her cheek. I flinch at first, but her touch is actually soothing and gives me a calming optimism. I savor every second of her hand on me and am disappointed when the moment ends all too quickly.

"Here, take this. There's no point in wrapping you up—you're just going to have to keep taking these when the pain gets bad. As long as there is nothing internally damaged, I think ribs heal up in a few weeks. I can't believe you hit the ground that hard, Max. Try falling a little more gracefully next time."

He hands me the pills—just plain acetaminophen, like that will do anything—and a bottle of water and turns his attention to Skylar.

"Okay Sky, let's have a look. Just go ahead and sit here first." He motions for her to take a seat on an old cut-down tree stump. Leaves crumble beneath their feet. I place the pills in my mouth and watch her as I open up the bottle of water. She pulls at her bottom lip with her teeth, something I notice her do often and that somehow, even covered in dirt and blood, makes me incapable of looking away. I swallow the water and pills as I listen to my dad talk about her wounds.

"This guy looks a lot worse than he really is. Here, let me

clean you off a little bit." He turns around to grab an antiseptic wipe and notices me still standing there staring. "How about you help Wiley keep watch, Max?"

I don't say anything as I grab my backpack and sling it over my shoulder, heading over to Wiley.

"See anything?"

"Nope, not really, just trees. But, look up there." He points in the distance to a large building. "I think we could probably find fuel up there."

I reply by saying, "I haven't checked yet, but we've probably traveled quite a distance away from the UTV. We might just have to give up on the idea of going back to refuel."

His face turns to complete disappointment. "Well, shit. What's the plan now then?"

"I hadn't thought that far, but I don't think going back is going to be the best option. We're all pretty banged up, so I think we should just keep moving forward. We might be able to find a vehicle up there in that parking lot." I point to the slightly vacant parking lot next to the building he pointed out. "There's a few vehicles, we could just hot-wire one of them."

Before we get much further in our discussion, Skylar and my dad walk up to join in. I look at Skylar and see that the majority of the blood that was once covering her cheek had been wiped away. She now has a bandage about the size of my palm covering quite a bit of her cheek. The rest of her face is speckled with little bits of dirt, but she still catches my eyes and gives me the sweetest and subtlest grin.

"What were you saying, Max?"

CHAPTER ELEVEN

MAX: Saturday, May 23

"Well, just that I don't think it's the best idea to keep searching for fuel and then backtrack to the UTV. As much as I loved that bad boy, I don't think it's worth traveling back for. We must have gone at least, like what, ten miles? I say we be happy that we're ten miles closer to the cabin. There's a building up there, and a few vehicles in the parking lot. Let's try to get one of those and make our way back on the road."

My dad looks at Wiley and Skylar. "Any objections?"

No one responds, so I take that as a no.

My dad continues. "Okay, sounds like a go. Let's follow the tree line just in case we need cover." He points ahead.

We begin walking in our normal formation. I'm not sure if it's the pain in my side heating my body, or I'm just now noticing what a hot day it is today, but I'm sweating like crazy. I raise my arm to wipe my face on my sleeve. After a few minutes, I begin to notice the others doing the same.

We walk half the distance to the building in silence. As we start approaching the building, I notice that the train we were traveling on has stopped next to the building. The car we were riding on appears to be past the building on the furthest side. I see the conductor's car closest to us.

I quietly say to the group, "Let's stop for a minute and check everything out from here."

We stop and hide within the trees as we dissect our surroundings. A few moments go by with no movement on or near the train. I begin to think that the train was on an automatic schedule, running by itself.

Just as we start to make our way out of the woods, I hear commotion coming up from behind us. It's voices. Angry voices, voices that I *don't* care to find out who they belong to.

My dad authoritatively says, "Guys, we need to run, NOW."

We take off running, the men behind us alerted to our presence. I try to remain in our normal formation but even through the pain I find myself passing Wiley. I urge him, "Pick up the pace Wiley!" Skylar runs at a pace close behind my dad but slows down to encourage Wiley to move faster.

"C'mon, Wiley, now isn't the time to let yourself slow down. I need you to run faster." She grabs onto his arm and begins to almost pull him. I turn slightly and see four men appear out of the trees behind us. They're fast. And they're gaining ground on us.

I hear one of the men shout to the others, "Secure all rebels!"

I have to process this statement a second longer to realize they were calling us the rebels. Shit. This can't be good. We need to get away from them ASAP.

I run faster, because death sounds worse than the shooting pain in my side, and pass my whole group. I grab the pistol that was holstered to my side and turn around in one swift motion, aiming at one of the men who shouts, "They're armed!"

Before they can draw their guns, I shoot and take down one of the men. Skylar and Wiley run past me. My dad stops running and comes back to stand by my side. We half walk, half run backward. I shoot at the men two more times, hitting one in the leg and missing the other. My dad draws his weapon and fires twice. His first shot is a miss, but his second takes down the man I hit in the leg.

My dad grabs my arm and says, "Come on. We need to keep moving."

We take off running and almost immediately catch up to Skylar and Wiley. As we start to run around the outside of the building, the men begin firing at us, forcing us to flee to the other side.

We're stuck.

We're stuck between this train and this building. The entrance of this building is at the end of this train, and I don't know what waits for us there, and I really don't want to find out. Our only option at this point is to try to escape between the train cars and hope we have a clear passing on the other side. I raise my arm behind myself and blindly fire another shot behind me in hopes to scare off the men, or at least slow them down.

I look at Skylar and say, "Okay, stay focused and follow me. Are you ready?"

"Yes."

"Right there," I say and point to an opening between train cars.

I pick up my pace and reach the opening before the others. I hop onto the gravel area surrounding the train tracks and initiate my path between the train cars. Dad is the first one to reach me. There is only room for one of us at a time, so I tell him to go ahead.

"Go through, get a plan."

Skylar is running as fast as she can, and Wiley is falling behind. The two remaining men are closing in on Wiley at a rapid pace. I raise my gun and wait for a clear shot, focusing on steadying my breathing as I close one eye to get a better aim.

Bang.

I shoot and take down the man that was closest to Wiley. I aim again as Skylar reaches me. I'm forced to switch positions to let her through. She squeezes by me. I fumble back into position after she passes and get back into the opening.

The man is within inches of Wiley. I have no open shot. Wiley reaches out, and I extend an arm for him to grab onto. Just as we make contact, the man lurches forward and grabs onto Wiley's bad ankle. Wiley lets out a terrified and painful scream.

I'm pulling him as hard as I can when more men start running towards us from the entrance of the building. All in the same black uniform.

Through Wiley's cries of pain, he screams, "Go! Protect her, Max!"

I can't let go. No matter how hard I pull I can't seem to make any progress on freeing him. The gravel slips beneath my feet. I step backward and pull him just slightly. The man continues to pull against Wiley. To my left, more men file out of the building. I pull him one more time as hard as I can and lose my grip.

I lose my grip on everything: his arm, my footing, my life.

I fall back as hard as I pulled on his arm and feel an incredible blunt force to the back of my head. I hear Skylar screaming, but I can't see her. I hear my dad yelling and firing his gun, but I can't see him. I can't see anything, and I can't move.

My whole world goes black.

I'm moving, but I can't open my eyes. I hear crying, but I can't speak.

All goes black.

I wake up to the sound of my mother singing. She always sung under her breath and hummed along to the radio. I hear her happily call, "Max, come down here sweetie." I sit up from my childhood bed and go to walk downstairs, feeling a strange déjà vu. The smell of her homemade chocolate chip cookies fills my lungs. We're at the cabin. I loved being here with her. We spent whole days just playing outside, going on little adventures. While I showered, she would always bake my favorite chocolate chip cookies.

"Max, come get a cookie while they're warm!"

I walk down the stairs and joy overwhelms me. I've missed this woman more than I could have ever imagined. Being able to see her again is all I've ever wanted. She looks up at me and smiles. "Honey, come get a cookie!"

I walk to the table and I hear more calling from a distance, "Max, Max, please, just come back to me Max."

All goes black.

My heart breaks. Six years is a terribly long time. I've missed her for six years. I was so close to being able to talk to her, hug her, tell her how I've missed her, to get her back just for a minute.

I hear crying, and I'm being pulled. The smell of grass completely erases the memory of the cookies. The pain I feel coursing through my body is immeasurable. My ribs are still on fire, and the pain in my head is a constant throb. I try to open my eyes, but they act as though they're permanently glued shut. I try to speak, but I can't muster a sound.

I hear Skylar's panicked voice. "Keith, I don't know how much further I can go. I can't carry him much more. We need to go back for Wiley, we have to go back." I hear her begin to sob again, and the pain of disappointment courses through my already completely pained body. I try to speak, to apologize, but I can't. I let her down. I failed them.

All goes black.

I'm being carried again. But this time it's with much more ease. I open my eyes to see my mom's beautiful face.

She looks down at me. "Shhh baby, almost to bed."

My heart is beyond full. We reach my bedroom, and she brings me inside. The posters and stencils on the walls make me believe I must be younger than six years old. The paint on the walls was from before my seventh birthday—when I decided I wanted plain blue paint instead of the childish cars and trucks stenciled on the walls.

She places me in bed gently and tucks me in. She sits there for a moment looking at me and whispers, "Max, you're my favorite little guy. Mommy loves you more than anything. You know you hold the biggest spot in Mommy's heart. Sleep tight, honey." She kisses my forehead.

I open my mouth to tell her to stay, to just sit with me for a while, but my mouth goes slack and no words come out. I feel a tear escape my eye as I try to hold back my emotions. I want nothing else but this moment to stay.

Instead, all goes black. I don't want to wake up this time. I don't want to hear anything, or see anything. I just want to rewind time to be back with my mom. She was my best friend, the most trusted person I've ever known, and she's gone, forever.

I could never forget the pain I felt when the cops came to tell my dad and me about the fate of the accident. We were hit so hard I was knocked unconscious immediately. I woke up in the hospital with my dad, who was anxiously sitting over my bed. I remember the doctors telling my dad that he would have to stay with me while my mom was in surgery. I remember the cops coming in to tell us that the man who hit us was over triple the legal limit of blood alcohol level. I remember the sound, the pain, that escaped my dad's throat when the doctors pulled him to the side to tell him that they lost my mother. That she was gone, that there was nothing they could do. She had suffered internal damages that couldn't be reversed.

The moment I knew I had lost my mother, I lost hope.

I want everything to fade to black.

The pain in my heart has overtaken the pain throughout my body.

I hear Skylar's voice, pleading to my dad. "I don't know what to do, Keith, what... you can't go."

With a stern voice he replies, "Skylar, listen to me. We can't stay under these football bleachers forever. I have to find somewhere safe for us to go for the night. We have to get him inside. His pulse is steady, but I need to check him over to see what's wrong. Skylar, put your gun in your hand and be ready if something happens. I will be back in no more than a half hour. Keep quiet and stay alert. Okay?"

Through muddled sobs, she must have shaken her head because I can hear him fumbling to get out from under the bleachers. I hear him try to walk quietly away.

Skylar whispers, "Max, please wake up. I...I can't do this without you. If you can hear me, please, just wake up."

I feel her hand caress the hair away from my brow. I realize my head is lying in her lap with the rest of me sprawled across the gravel beneath this bleacher. My body aches. My head pulsates as the pain amplifies. As I start to fade to black, I'm brought back by her voice. "Please don't leave me. You told me you would be here to protect me, Max. I've already lost Wiley, I can't lose you, too."

A teardrop falls from her face onto my cheek. It's warm,

and as it begins to slide down my cheek, she wipes it away. I feel her bring herself closer. Her face is extremely close to mine, and I can feel her warm breath against my cheek. Lemon and lavender.

"Please...Max, wake up." I feel her lean even closer and she unexpectedly places her lips delicately against mine. My heart skips a beat and butterflies flood my stomach. I want so badly to just wake up, to kiss her, to tell her I'm here, but I can't. The moment is gone too soon as she takes her lips slightly off mine.

She mutters against them, "You promised," and everything disappears to black.

CHAPTER TWELVE

WILEY: Saturday, May 23

This is bad, really, really, bad.

I can't see. I try, but there's something over my eyes, some kind of blindfold. When the lights are on, I can see a faint brightness, but most of the time the lights are off, and it's pure darkness. I have to rely on all of my other senses.

My hands are tied with zip ties, and I've tried so desperately to remember that self-defense special I saw on the news about how to get out of kidnapping situations, but I can't for the life of me remember the actual advice.

God, I'm going to die here. My stomach churns, both from hunger and fear.

But, why haven't they killed me yet? Are they going to torture me?

I take in a deep breath. There is a faint smell of cigarettes and burnt coffee.

I tug at my wrists. Multiple zip ties dig into me, like zip ties on zip ties. It's a fucking puzzle.

My legs are zip tied, too. Which is awesome, cause, ya know, it's not like my ankle hurts or anything. Even if I wanted to try to break my legs free, I'm too much of a baby to do it through the nagging pain.

The sound of the door immediately stops my fidgeting. I try to open my eyes wide when I see the brightness appear.

"Hello?"

Nothing. Just the cautious sound of feet as they approach.

As the figure gets closer, so does the smell of sweat and cigarettes. The person kneels and sets something on the ground.

"I...need to assess your wound."

A doctor?

"Can you help me? Can you please untie me?"

"If you can't stay still, I'll have to sedate you again. Please... just cooperate."

Again?

"Please, no please, please just...I won't say anything. Can I just go? I won't cause any trouble."

I hear him fumbling with his instruments and panic washes over me.

"Sir, please, I won't. Just let me go. I haven't seen anything..." But before I can get my final "please" in, I feel something cold pierce my neck, and I drift away.

Sometime later, I awake to the sound of two men chatting in the doorway. There is only a faint amount of brightness, I assume from the hallway. I don't move. I just listen as intently as possible.

"We need to interrogate him, gather as much intel as possible before."

"I understand."

"He may be with the resistance."

"Or he could not, he could just be with family, fleeing, like everyone else we've captured."

"They had weapons, James."

"And they were sloppy. Those men in the Sanchez regiment were trained and knew what they were doing."

"All I'm saying, is it's worth a shot. If we're going to do this, we have to have full control. We can't fail this time."

"The search is still going for the rest of his group. We're actively tracking them."

Thank God, they haven't found them yet.

"I'll get him to talk."

"Just try not to kill this one."

I swallow the lump that's formed in my throat. I'm not strong enough for this, I'm going to die.

CHAPTER THIRTEEN

MAX: date unknown

I don't know how long I've been in the darkness, but I'm surprised to feel myself being carried again. My legs drag over the ground, and I want so much to just lift them and walk by myself, but I can't bring my body to do anything I want.

I hear my dad say, "There's a house, just across the football field; that's where we're going. We should be safe there for a few days. I only came across one other person, but I was forced to take him down. These people... they're so...violent. It's like all normal human behavior has been ripped away from them and replaced with constant aggression. Sky, you haven't said a word since I got back. Are you okay?"

She sniffles and responds, "Are you talking about the blue house up ahead?"

"Yeah."

I begin to fade again, but I don't allow myself the pleasure. I feel the pavement beneath us change as we cross over what I assume to be a street or alleyway. It then switches over to grass. We go another few feet and my dad says, "Go ahead and open the door. I already secured the house. Just open the door, and then help me get him inside."

I feel so helpless, so worthless. My body is brought up two steps and into the house. The air is cool and crisp inside, not like the humid, sticky hotness outside. My body begins to relax as I let the coolness take over. I feel myself being lowered onto a couch. A pillow is placed behind my head, my legs lifted onto the couch.

Skylar asks, "What do we do now?"

I begin to fade again, and no matter how hard I try, I can't control it this time. The darkness overcomes me.

When I come back, I feel fully rested. I assume I'm in one of those halfway stages of consciousness I've been stuck in but decide to try to open my eyes anyway. I'm relieved when I feel them open. There's darkness, but not the type of darkness I've grown used to. It's the type when the sun has gone down and the moon is the only light illuminating the room. I focus on trying to move my hands. I don't want to make any sudden movements, so I start with one finger. It's a success. I wiggle it around a few times to confirm my movement.

I stare at the ceiling, wiggling my finger. I don't want to wait any longer. I use the force of my wiggling hand to bring myself up off my back to a sitting position.

I hear Skylar suddenly jerk awake. "Oh my God, Max, you're back, thank God."

I didn't realize she was sleeping in a chair right next to me.

She shouts across the room, "Keith, wake up, Max is...awake!"

She comes closer and places her hand on my back as she kneels beside me. "Max, you should probably lie back down." I look at her confused, trying to comprehend what has happened and begin to feel myself become dizzy.

My dad rushes over and gently pushes me back into a lying position. "Whoa, whoa, not so fast. You can sit up but not so sudden. You've been lying there for about eight hours now. Give yourself a minute to catch up."

Through my cracking voice, I manage to say, "I need something to drink." Skylar reaches for a bottle of water sitting on the table and takes off the lid. She helps lift my head slightly and pours a little bit of water into my mouth. I allow myself to savor the thirst-quenching relief of the water before swallowing.

I mutter, "Thank you."

I take another drink of the water to satisfy my thirst, then ask, "What happened?"

My dad clears his throat as he begins, "Well, Max, a lot did."

He points to Skylar and says, "Skylar and I had to drag your body about a half of a mile to hide under a football bleacher...then I had to leave her to find this house. Luckily she was capable enough to wait with you and help me get you here."

"But, what happened before that? Why was I out so long?"

"Buddy, you took a heck of a hit to the back of the head. I knew you were knocked out, but I honestly didn't know for how long, or if you would even come back to us."

"Wait." As I begin to sit up I feel for the knot on the back of my head. "I think I remember. Oh God, where's Wiley?"

I look at both of them, and their chins both drop to their chests.

I repeat myself in a sterner voice. "Tell me where he is."

Another moment goes by before my dad clears his throat again. "Max, you did everything you could. You nearly killed yourself trying to save him. There was nothing we could do... they took him. We were lucky to get away."

"Wait, they took him? He's still alive and you didn't go back for him?" I...remember hearing her say we should go back for him. Why... "This is all my fault." I turn to her and say desperately, "Skylar, I'm so sorry," and then turn to him. "Dad, we have to go back."

"Max, it would be a complete suicide mission to go back now," he says in a low mundane tone. "We need to keep moving forward—that's what Wiley would have wanted. We have no idea of their intentions, or capabilities. Not to mention that none of us are in the best condition."

My irritation grows, and I can't sit here any longer. I push myself onto my feet and immediately get a head rush. I'm unstable and fall back down. The back of my head begins to throb, and I wince as the sharp pain in my torso reminds me of my bruised ribs.

I sit there for a minute listening to the thumping of my headache. I don't want to seem like a coward, but I can't even think straight with this pain.

I ask, "Pain killers?"

My dad pushes a prescription medicine bottle across the table. "Whoever lived here must have had surgery or something —just take half of one, for now, to see how it affects you."

I grab the bottle and examine the words on the side. *Disp: Hydrocodone/APAP 5/500mg, Generic for: Vicodin 5/500mg.* I think to myself, as I look at the name on the bottle, *Thank you very much, Meadows, B.* Skylar hands me the bottle of water she had helped me get a drink from, and with one swift drink, I swallow down my sweet relief. I'm happy to see that the pill bottle is mostly full. I toss it back to my dad and say, "We should probably borrow that just in case."

He replies back, "Yep, that's what I was thinking. Never

know when you'll hurt yourself again." He smirks a little and says, "I'm surprised you didn't dent that railroad track you landed on. Hadn't I just told you that you need to learn to fall more gracefully?" He turns away and walks out of the room.

I feel the back of my head again and my mind flashes to just earlier today, losing grip on his arm and falling. I must have landed on the set of railroad tracks parallel to the ones we had hopped over to escape. My stomach sinks, and an immense feeling of failure courses through me, knowing that I couldn't keep my grip and pull him through. I feel sick that I let Skylar down, and that I wasn't there for her. I flash back to the sound of her voice telling me to come back, that she needed me. A flush goes across my body as I remember the feeling of her lips placed against mine.

Skylar's voice interrupts my thoughts. "Are you okay?"

I hadn't even realized that I had raised my hand to my lips in remembrance of her kiss. I lower my hand, but the feeling of my fingertips lingers on my lips, or maybe that was the memory of her lips on mine. What if the memory of her lips was merely a figment of my imagination, like those of my childhood with my mother? My heart aches as I remember being so close to my mom and not being able to tell her how deeply I miss her.

I manage to reply with a simple, "Yeah."

I look at her face for the first time since I've awoken—really look at her face. I see a broken girl, with dirt-grazed skin and messy hair. She looks like she hasn't gotten any rest herself.

I grow curious, so I ask her, "What did you do while I was out?"

She looks away, fumbling with her fingers, searching for an answer. She doesn't look up but admits cautiously, "I couldn't... ugh...leave your side. I just had to keep hoping that you would wake up, and I wanted to be there when you did."

I understand completely, but I don't know why she would choose this.

I'm at a loss for words. I continue to examine her, and although she's almost facing away, I see a single tear roll across her cheek and fall into her lap. I'm reminded of the tear landing on my cheek in my memory of earlier. I place my fingertips on the spot to savor the feeling. I lower my hand from my cheek and reach out to place it on top of her delicate hand.

She looks up to me slowly. "Come here," I say.

Her eyes glisten as she moves from the chair next to the couch, the one that she had been posted on for the day, to the seat beside me on the couch. I don't take my hand or eyes off of her as she moves.

She sits down next to me, without saying a word. I raise my arm to place it around her shoulders and pull her to me. She doesn't resist, and lays her head on my shoulder. I take my other arm to pull her closer as I wrap my arms around her. It hurts to hold her like this, physically, because of how tender my side is, but I fight through and rest my cheek on the top of her head and mutter the words, "I'm sorry...I let you down."

We sit there in silence for a while. I hear my dad fumbling with papers in the other room but don't bother to check in on what he's doing. He seems more level headed than I am at the moment, and right now, all I want to do is sit here with Skylar. I feel her arms go limp as she falls asleep, so I free my right arm to recline the couch.

The noise from the recliner prompts my dad to stop fumbling around and come back into the living room. He pauses in the doorway as he sees us. He walks over to the other couch and without saying a word, grabs a fleece blanket. He walks over and covers us both up. My dad whispers, "I don't think that girl has slept at all. Get some sleep. We'll regroup in the morning."

He turns and walks back out of the room, and before a minute goes by, he's back to fumbling with the papers again. I shut out his sounds and focus on Skylar's breathing: in and out, slow and steady. I find myself pleased that she was finally at ease enough to fall asleep in my arms. I don't want to let this moment go, but I can't help it as I'm being taken over by not only exhaustion and pain medicine but also the rhythm of her breathing. I feel Skylar's arm move and tighten across my waist as she nestles in closer to me. I tilt my head to the side and give the top of her head a gentle kiss.

I don't want to fade away; I want to stay.

CHAPTER FOURTEEN

KEITH: Sunday, May 24

I can finally focus better now that I know Max is conscious. I didn't know how long he would be out, and with head injuries, I was worried. I tend to be able to block things out, and focus on what needs to be done, and that's what I've been doing. It's what I've had to do. To keep everyone safe, to figure out what's happening.

What *is* happening?

Deep breath. Okay. Let me think about what I know, what I don't know, and what I need to know.

The paperwork hasn't been helpful. I know it will be, I know Sam wouldn't have wanted me to take it unless it would help me figure things out. Unless I took the wrong thing, maybe I read his code wrong. Sam was smart, I don't know why he didn't come to me with this and let me help him. What did he get himself into that he couldn't trust me with it?

I shift my focus back to the task at hand, gathering and processing data. So, we know that the virus impacts people in a manner that makes them batshit crazy. Mean as hell. Vicious. But why? The report said bio-weapon and mind-control.

The virus was spread via our water supply. That was documented in the paperwork. Whoever *they* are, found a way to bypass the filtration system, so all public water sources nearby that were accessible were contaminated. I wonder if the mind-control actually worked, or if all that resulted were side-effects? A bad reaction?

The report also stated flu-like symptoms, which explains the epidemic that has been going around. Is that also a side-effect, or a precursor to whatever was next? Does everyone get the flu symptoms?

So much of the report is redacted, and I desperately wish I could just see the whole thing. There was a mention of this organism not to be used with other things, is that possibly where things went wrong?

There's a list I haven't figured out yet. Cities...with no other information. *Columbus, Houston, Los Angeles, Salt Lake City, Seattle, Denver, Minneapolis, St. Louis, New Orleans, Tampa, and Washington.* Is this their bases? Their suppliers? Their targets?

I feel like all I do is spin my wheels. I need to figure one solid thing out.

I need a blood sample.

Sigh.

I get up and walk over to the window. I've done this at least a dozen times, just peeping outside at whatever might be out there. I study the surroundings cautiously, as to not open the blinds covering the window too much, giving away our hiding place.

I've seen them, the angry people. The first time I looked

outside was because I heard a loud noise and couldn't place it. I lightly fingered the blinds just enough to see outside and saw a man, nearly six-foot, close to my height, pounding his fists against a mailbox. It was so strange, to see someone behave in this manner, to watch from a distance far enough away to be safe, but close enough to see his inhumane motions.

Seeing that man wreak such havoc disturbed me, but also intrigued me to know how and why this is happening. I want to understand the science behind it, and the goal the mystery men had in mind.

What else I'd like to make sense of is why these crazy ass people stop being lunatics at night. I kept watching, on and off, and they seem to go into some sort of dormant stage at night. The people are still out there, and active, but it's sporadic and not nearly like what we've witnessed during the day.

I also desperately want to know that Wiley is okay. That guy is like a brother to me. Or maybe a son. Man, that guy is ditzy. He means well, I know he does, but he relies on me too much, and I'm worried without me what will happen.

Last week, he was vacuuming his house, and had plugged the vacuum into the same area his portable AC unit was and blew the breaker. No big deal, but he called me at work to ask what happened to his power. I guess I just assume all men know their way around a breaker box.

Don't get me wrong though, he's been there his fair share for me. When Maura died, I lost nearly everything. I lost the will to live for a while. Wiley made sure to keep me company and keep me fed, while helping out with Max. He's pretty much a second dad to Max after that rough patch. I really don't know if I would have made it through all of that without him. And now, it turns my stomach to not know if he's okay.

I close my eyes and try to calm my mind from thinking just for a moment. *Think happy thoughts*, I tell myself. *Relax, calm your mind,* that's what Maura would have said. I let my mind be as open and empty as possible, until I hear a voice coming from the other room.

The kids must be awake. Now there's another mystery I don't have time to figure out.

CHAPTER FIFTEEN

MAX: Sunday, May 24

For the first time in a while, I don't dream. I wake, feeling fully rested, to see the sun peeking through the windows, and I almost forget where I am for a moment. I doubt the reality of my sleeping situation when I look down and see this beautiful girl still fast asleep on my chest. I don't want to taint the perfection of my reality, but I know we need to get going with our day.

I look down at her and gently move away the strand of hair that fell over her face. I study her features—the curve of her nose, the bow-like shape of her just-full-enough lips, the soft yet defined jawline. I sneak another kiss to her forehead, and as I remove my lips, she begins to wake up. At first, she's calm but then immediately sits up to say, "Oh, um, crap, I—ugh, didn't mean to fall asleep. I'm—ugh, sorry."

I sit up slowly as to not cause myself to go dizzy again and say gently, "It's fine. I enjoyed it. I mean, I was comfortable and fell asleep, too." She shoots me a worried glance, so I assure her, "Really, Skylar. I was more than okay with the sleeping situation."

She begins to relax and jokingly says, "I hope I didn't drool on you." She wipes at her face.

I laugh slightly and am reminded of my sore ribs. I have to grab my side and Skylar says, "Crap, see, I'm sorry, hold on and I'll find that pain medicine."

I immediately release my side and force myself to forget the pain. "No, you're fine." I muster a smile and say, "I'm fine, everything's fine. It just caught me off guard."

Just then my dad walks in the room and sarcastically says, "Max, did you hurt yourself again?"

"Oh, you know, just old injuries," I say lightly. "Do you have that Vicodin?"

"Yep, let me grab it. How did you do with it? Do you want half or one?"

"I fell asleep so I'm not sure, I'll just stick with half for now. Don't wanna pass out and make you two carry me again."

He jokes back, "You're a lot heavier than you look."

Tension builds in the room as I switch the conversation back to serious matters. "What were you doing last night? I heard you messing around with papers most of the night."

"Oh, I was just..." as he walks out of the room.

He comes back a few seconds later and hands me the pain pill and continues, "I was looking over some of the paperwork I have. Nothing seems to make much sense."

He looks puzzled as he starts to say, "But I was also doing a little research on what's going on around us. I've been watching out the windows. After we got here, I wanted to make sure we were alone. I saw a few of those indignant folks wandering around a few houses down. Every so often I would go check to see where they went or if they were still there. For a while, they would wander around, and aimlessly start beating random objects: cars, mailboxes, front doors, whatever they could. But then, when the sun went down, and nightfall hit, they became much less aggressive. Almost like they were dormant."

My need for water breaks his deliberation slightly as I click the recliner back into its upright position and stand up. He continues, so I try to be quiet as I scour the room for a bottle of water to take my pain reliever. Skylar reads my mind and hands me a bottle.

"I know this sounds crazy, but I think whatever drives them to act so violent escapes them at night. I don't know if it's like an internal clock type thing, or temperature change, or something to do with sunlight or their vision; I haven't figured that out yet. But I feel like this is a step closer to figuring out what we're up against."

"Okay, so let me see if I'm following here. The clan of pissed off people who wish to beat us to death go into a slumber at nightfall?"

"Well, I haven't seen them actually lie down and take a nap, I'm just saying, they aren't as aggressive at night. As soon the sun came up this morning, I saw them start to get more destructive and hostile."

I let this sink in for a minute, and an alarming question that I'm not really sure why just now hits me, comes to mind. "Well, what's stopping us from turning into one of those people? I mean, look around. We can't be the only sane people left on this planet. Either we're complete savages, or we run around in black uniforms shooting at people and taking them hostage?"

"Trust me, Max, this isn't the first time I've thought about this. I don't know what's setting us apart from the others, but I'm sure glad for whatever it is. I do know, whatever we do, we shouldn't drink, or even let the tap water touch us. The reports

I read stated whatever was being manufactured in our lab was being dumped into the water supply."

I look down at the bottle of water in my hand and examine the contents. My dad cuts my thoughts off as if reading my mind. "I feel confident that bottled spring water will be fine for consumption. I doubt that they had the authority or power to go all the way to wherever that spring water is from and contaminate it without someone stopping them. Oh, and well water should be fine, another reason we need to get to the cabin sooner than later; a hot shower would be nice."

Skylar becomes alert and says, "Have you checked the TV?"

"Yeah, last night I tried, but all the lines are down, just static."

"Maybe..." she says as she starts fumbling through her backpack. "Ahh, here it is," she says while holding up her cell phone.

I joke and say, "You need to make a status update or something?"

"Very funny, Max, but maybe social media feeds will load from prior to everything shutting down."

"We checked earlier, remember?"

"Yeah, well, it's worth a try, right? Maybe the old feeds will load?"

My dad speaks up and says, "Yeah I actually hadn't thought of that. Good thinkin', Sky."

It annoys me a little when my dad calls her "Sky." Sometimes it reminds me of the nightmare I had in the woods where her accomplice called her Sky. But maybe it's not the name itself, just the fact that he feels comfortable enough to have a nickname for her. I want a "nickname" type relationship with her, too. I begin to feel like a toddler who doesn't want to share.

It's my dad, and it's Skylar; I don't need to feel jealous.

"I think the battery died. It'll usually stay on for a couple minutes before dying again."

We all huddle together trying to look at the small cell phone screen. The welcome greeting song plays as the phone boots up. My palms begin to sweat as I think about whatever may be looming around social media. Has the whole world become corrupted? Or just our state? Did people make it a point to post an update that they were turning into crazy people? Are there others out there in our position?

Before I can think anything else, her phone beeps loudly, and a message flashes across the screen: *Emergency Alert System – A rapid pandemic has flushed through our nation, and we are ordering all people capable of reading this message to immediately report to your local health department, hospital, or police station. A vaccination will be given as a proper immunization protocol against this virus. Please refrain from contact with any person experiencing erratic behavior or those in lethargic or comatose conditions.*

As soon as she finished reading the message out loud, her phone powers down. That was it.

We're all quiet for a minute until Skylar speaks up. "Lethargic? Comatose? What?... So, we should go, right? To get the shot and be safe?"

I look from Skylar's questioning face and turn to my dad. I don't think he realizes but he's caressing his chin with his hand, in a very deep thought process.

I interrupt him by saying, "Dad?"

He pauses for a minute. "I don't think that was legit."

He stops for another second and begins again. "I mean, obviously it was a legit message, but I don't think it's what it seems to be. The message was sloppy. Not as professional as the alerts typically are. I think it's a ploy to get the unaffected to target areas to do what they please with them. And the more I think about it, why wasn't the alert broadcasted on TV? Maybe the cell towers were easier to breach."

I challenge his theory by saying, "Or the person who wrote the alert was in a hurry, considering all around us. There's a logical excuse for all of those scenarios."

He rubs his forehead as if it helps him think. "I'm not buying it. Whoever is responsible for the epidemic, the shootings, Wiley's abduction—I think that's who made this message. And the whole lethargic thing, what is that? The only people we've seen have been deranged."

Hearing Wiley's name cuts deep, and the guilt I feel for his abduction grows. I know we can't be far from where everything happened, and if I could only convince them to stay here another night, maybe I could leave at night and get him. I'll complain my head and body aren't feeling well enough for travel yet. I have to do something or I won't be able to live with myself. And with the new knowledge of the people being less angry at night, I might have a better chance.

Skylar speaks up again and says, "Well, we really haven't seen too many people, so who knows what all reactions have happened."

I say, "Right," in agreement. I turn to my dad and say, "So, what should we do then, Dad?"

"I don't know yet. I need to think for a little bit."

Perfect timing.

"Well, it may not be too bad of an idea to wait to leave here until tonight," I suggest. "That way when we leave, those things outside won't be so mad. Might give us safer travels." I say this out loud with the intention of canceling our plan at the last minute by way of headache and postponing until just before dawn. That should give me plenty of time to sneak out while they're asleep.

I'm going after Wiley. I want to include them in on this, but

I know neither one of them would go through with it. Skylar might but I don't want her to risk getting hurt again over my mistake.

I feel uneasy with the uncertainty of how far this plague has stretched. And now, with my head filled with my dad's disbelief of the message, I can't help but wonder who is in control, and why?

My dad replies, "Yeah, we should probably take the day to get things in order and rest up for tonight. I'm going to go look through the paperwork again to see if I can uncover anything I missed." He points to the counter. "There's some breakfast over there. Not much to choose from, but at least we won't go hungry. Make sure you're only drinking bottled drinks. Whatever you do, stay away from the tap."

Skylar and I munch out on the food that my dad found in the kitchen. We joke about our gourmet selection and take turns sharing. She hands me her other Pop-Tart, and for a second, I forget about how horrible the world has become and enjoy the carefree time I'm lucky enough to share with her. We finish eating, and as I gather the rest of what remains I tell her, "Let's split this between our backpacks for later."

"Good idea, I'll go grab them."

She pulls the backpacks onto the couch, and I start finding places to stash the food inside. A pack of crackers here, a granola bar there. She's kneeling on the couch holding the backpacks open as I stand next to the arm on the side facing her. I finish and we both look up at the same time, making eye contact. My eyes retract from hers to the horrible bruise on her cheek. She must have noticed the movement of my eyes and facial expression when she says defensively, "Is it that bad?"

I immediately say, "It's just, I feel so responsible for it. I feel horrible. You have no idea how bad I feel. I'm sorry."

I reach out and place my hand against her cheek slightly.

She closes her eyes and moves her hand up to hold my hand against her face. The warmth of her touch surges through my body. I can't help myself when I take my free hand and place it on the other side of her face below her chin, against her neck.

I don't think, I just do. I do what my body aches for. I lean down and inch my face closer and closer to hers, just stopping as our noses touch. I slide my hand further around the back of her neck to grasp her. I feel her breath against mine growing unsteady. I don't know what she's thinking; I can only wish I knew. The only thing I know right now is the intense desire I have to press my lips against hers. My heart sputters, and I can't fight the urge any longer. I do what I've wanted to do for too long.

She kisses me back, slowly at first and then more passionately. Every inch of my body surges and awakens with desire. I take one hand and place it on the small of her back to bring her closer to me. I feel her delicate hands on me, too, reaching up on my neck to pull me closer. She brings one hand up and runs it deeply through my hair. The way her lips fit effortlessly against mine only makes me believe that they were meant to be together.

I have to pull myself away, to allow us to catch our breaths. I rest my forehead against hers and savor the moment. Somehow, still lavender.

"Max...you just...you just can't do that," she says as she pulls away completely.

"Are you telling me you didn't want that, Skylar?" My feelings and ego are a little crushed. I was under the impression that we were having a mutual connection, especially the way she kissed me back.

"You just shouldn't...I just shouldn't have...I can't..." She doesn't finish as she gets up to walk away.

"You need to tell me what I did wrong Skylar, don't just

walk away." I begin to grow frustrated and raise my tone, "You have to let your guard down, please, just let me in."

She turns around, and with tears welling in her eyes, she musters, "I can't, Max."

I can't even see straight I'm so aggravated. Here I am, about to pour my heart out to this girl, and she basically shuts me out completely. Typical Skylar. She doesn't care who she hurts, as long as she's the one calling the shots.

I grab my backpack and gun off the coffee table and shout, "Fine, push me out and I'll be gone." I walk to the same back door we entered through yesterday and turn the handle. A small part of me tries to talk myself out of leaving, but the majority of myself is saying now or never. I turn the handle and walk out into the world. The humidity smacks me right in the face and reminds me of the ever-changing weather this time of year. I slam the door shut and before anyone can stop me, I take off running.

CHAPTER SIXTEEN

SKYLAR: Sunday, May 24

He kissed me. The searing yet sweet feeling of his lips on mine burn deep into my memory. It was perfect, it was everything I wanted it to be.

But I can't. I can't let him in.

I can't let him see how truly broken I am.

The broken family, the anxiety, the insomnia, the unhealthy relationships with nearly every single person, the learned patterns of negative thinking I can't seem to break.

He won't understand, even if he says he could.

I don't want to hurt him, but my desire to not be hurt is stronger. This will be better for him anyway. It has to be. Right?

He deserves someone who is happy, who loves herself and won't constantly worry if she's good enough or if he'd stay.

But what if he would? What if he would love me, and help me even though I feel so helpless? It's a burden I don't think any other person should have to handle.

But what if?

The way he looks at me like I'm the only girl in the world—his sweet, and soft way he handles me, like I'm this precious thing to him—our history together, the real history—the way I feel when he's around, safe and cared for—even the way he annoys me, and the way he reacts when I drive him crazy. It fits. It's dysfunctional, and I know he has issues and maybe, just maybe, we could be there for each other despite those.

But, maybe we can't, and maybe I could spare us the gory details of whatever could have happened. I have to do this.

CHAPTER SEVENTEEN

MAX: Sunday, May 24

I have no plan. I haven't thought any of this through, and that scares me, but it also makes me feel more alive than ever. I try to retrace my unconscious steps. I vaguely remember being carried for a while, through a football field. I look around as I'm running and spot the bleachers I assume I was under with Skylar. My mind shifts to hearing her plead for me to come back to her, that she couldn't do this alone. *She lied.* She pleaded for me to come back to her, and put her lips against mine, and she lied.

I reach the bleachers without looking back.

I slow down at the bleachers to assess where I need to be going. In the distance, I see a set of railroad tracks. I know if I reach those, I can travel north to get back to the building where Wiley was taken. As I'm surveying my surroundings, a person in the distance catches my eye.

And then more people appear. There seems to be a herd of

them gathering on the football field. I quickly realize I'm going to have to backtrack around the high school to get around them. I take off running, and as I do, I make sure my gun is loaded.

The sound of the bullet being loaded into the chamber is a sound that had once startled me but now sets me at ease. I start to think about how horrible this plan is, that I should probably just go back, but the stubbornness I'm experiencing won't let me turn around empty-handed.

I make my way towards the school, trying to be aware of everything around me. I round the corner and am stopped dead in my tracks by another herd of people. I don't think they've noticed that I'm here, so I slowly retreat backward. I turn around slowly, and as I begin to make my descent, a woman comes from out of nowhere.

Before I can react, she hits me forcefully in the jaw and knocks me off balance. I stumble and she rears her leg up and kicks me with another blunt force to the side. With my previous injuries, I can't risk letting her hit me again. I draw my gun up, and just as she is about to unleash another brutal kick, a gunshot brings her to the ground. I look behind where the woman has fallen, and there stands Skylar with her gun in her hands.

With her gun still raised and ready to shoot, she motions for me to come over, and as much as I despise her right now, I do as she says. When I reach her, she says, "You're an idiot. What were you thinking?"

I respond hastily, "Does it even matter Skylar? You don't seem to care about anything else, why would you want to know what I was thinking?"

She glares at me, as if giving me the silent treatment now.

"If you must know, I was going to try to go back."

"Back where?"

"To Wiley."

"Oh," she says, sounding surprised and confused.

I confess. "I planned on doing it tonight, after you two went to sleep. But with the current situation, I figured what the heck, I could use some fresh air anyways."

"As much as I want to do the same thing, it's just not the smartest option right now, Max. We need to keep moving."

"You sound like my dad brainwashed you, Skylar. This is your family we're talking about."

"Yeah, *my* family. And I'm pretty sure *my* family wouldn't want me risking my life with no plan whatsoever."

My dad appears from around the corner. He gives me a "get your ass over here" type of look. I don't want to waste any more time, so I quickly make my way over, and he scolds me: "What were you thinking, Max? This world is not the same. Do *not* ever do something like that again. We're going back to the house now and packing up for tonight." He doesn't even give me time to respond as he shouts, "Now!"

Not a word is spoken on the run back to the house. We enter the backyard and make sure no one had followed us as we enter the back door. My dad slams his gun on the counter. "Now what exactly happened there? And I'm talking to both of you. This type of behavior can't happen again. Either choose to get along or agree to disagree. This constant bickering between you two is getting old. I can't keep being the mediator. You two need to figure your shit out. But you have to wait until after we figure out what the hell is going on. These types of risks can't be taken under our circumstances. Christ, Max, you haven't even healed from your head or rib injury."

"I know, I'm sorry. I just needed some air. I needed to get away for a minute."

Skylar tilts her head to the side and squints her eyes slightly, looking dead at me as if to make me feel guilty about not telling my dad the truth; the truth that I was going on a potential suicide rescue mission.

He begins again in his disappointed tone. "Now isn't the time. We all need some air, you're not the only one. You just need to realize that you're going to have to put your own crap on hold right now. When we reach the cabin, I don't care what you do. Go frolic in the woods for all I care, but right now, you have got to keep your head in the game. Understand me?"

I feel like a scolded puppy with my tail in between my legs. But, he's right. I don't know why I let her bother me, but I've got to shut it down. Whatever we have together—Skylar and I—it isn't healthy.

I say to him, but I make eye contact with her, "Yeah, I understand."

He replies, "Good, now reload your gun, and make sure your things are packed. We'll have plenty of ammo to get us to the cabin, but you need to be paying attention to reloading. I have a few more things to do, then we need to rest before we go. Can I trust you two to stay inside the house this time?"

We nod, and he walks out of the room. The tension between me and Skylar thickens the air. I maintain my eye contact with her, and say quietly enough for my dad not to hear but loud enough to make my point to her, "Whatever this is"—I point back and forth through the space between us—"it's no more."

She interrupts me by saying, "Max, don't do this right now."

"I'm not doing it ever. I'm just making it clear to you. I'm done. You've made me aware of what a fool I am. You duped me, Skylar. I regret ever thinking there was something between us."

She goes to open her mouth, and I cut her off. "You don't

need to make excuses. I don't want to hear them. You've made your point, and now I've made mine."

Before I can say anything else, sounds from outside bring me to a halt. I hear a vehicle. *Can these demented people still drive?* My dad arrives back in the living room without a sound and motions for Skylar and me to join him in kneeling beside the couch. A voice appears from outside and shouts, "We know you're here. We heard the gunshot. Come outside now, and we'll take you to our headquarters." He pauses momentarily and says again, "We will find you. You can either come out or we'll come looking. We can protect you, just come with us."

The sound of the vehicle passes our house slowly. The road is only about a half-mile with around a dozen houses. My dad speaks up but remains hushed. "Grab your stuff, but do it quietly. We're going to have to make a run for it."

Skylar contradictorily says, "Why can't we just raise our white flag and go with them?"

My dad wide-eyes Skylar. "Skylar, don't be so closed-minded. These are the same guys who poisoned our population, shot at us, and kidnapped your uncle. Do *not* believe anything they say. We are not safe. You have to trust me on this. We're better off on our own."

She doesn't bother to respond but gets up to get her backpack. I do the same. My dad rushes back to his makeshift office. Within a few moments, he surges back in and asks, "Ready?"

I nod my head in agreement and he says, "Remember, keep your head in the game."

He takes a quick peek out of the front window blinds and tells us, "All right. We get to the woods, we're safe." He turns and with a solemn face speaks, "I can't stress this enough: stay focused. Gun in hand, ready to fire if they approach. Formation is me, Skylar, and then you, Max, you'll follow up the rear." He points to me. "Do not hesitate."

"All right guys, they're almost to the end of the block. One...two... Let's go!"

My heart races as Dad slowly turns the doorknob. As subtly as possible he opens the door. The door creaks, and before we can muffle the sound, the men at the end of the street spot us. My dad yells at us, "Now!" as he takes off running. Skylar and I take off after him. I turn to see the men speeding towards us in their SUV. I hear a gunshot, and before I can comprehend, I see the dirt a few feet to my right fly up into the air. *They're shooting at me!* I'm not close enough to shoot productively, so I just raise my gun and fire their direction anyway. My eyes catch something in my peripheral—a group of the deranged running toward the SUV.

I hear a loud thud, and I look over my shoulder to see a body being run over by the SUV. The person must have leaped onto the vehicle and then fell off. The sound of the body being crumpled sickens me but doesn't slow me down. I hear another gunshot—this time the bullet hits the ground right near Skylar. I'm brought back to my defense and react by shooting another two bullets near the SUV. One makes contact with the front passenger tire and blows it completely out. The SUV drives another few feet until the men give up and take off after us on foot.

I catch up to Skylar and urge her, "Faster!"

I look ahead and see the tree line closing in. I hear more gunshots and start running in erratic zig-zags to try to throw off the gunmen. Each step sends fireballs of pain shooting through me. My dad is the first to reach the woods. I don't take my eyes off of his path as Skylar and I follow closely behind. We hop over fallen trees and large rocks. The gap between us and the men begins to grow. I can still hear them, but they've lost the proximity to shoot at us. I feel my headache growing and try to block out the fierce pain radiating from my side.

My dad points and says, "There, we have to cross there."

It's a creek bed around fifty yards wide. There's a quick incline and what I assume to be a drop off. If we can get to the other side before they cross, we can lose them easily.

The creek is lined with trees, so my dad runs to the most hidden area and begins to make his way across. Skylar hesitates when she reaches the water. I reach her side and tell her, "Holster your gun, grab my hand." She continues to hesitate and I urge her, "Now Skylar, just take my hand."

I won't break my promise; I will do everything I can to keep her safe.

She reaches back to holster her gun while I turn to evaluate the distance we have between these men. I grab her hand and tell her, "Watch your footing, these rocks will be slippery. I won't let you fall, but we really need to move fast."

My dad has already cleared half of the creek bed with ease. The water is around knee depth but is rushing pretty rapidly. I feel myself almost lose my footing and quickly regain stability.

Skylar's grip on my hand is so firm that I begin to think I may lose circulation if we don't reach the edge soon. My dad reaches the end of the creek as we hit the middle point. He turns around and tells us, "Pick up the pace."

I watch as he raises his gun and then I am distracted by the gunfire a few feet to my right. I'm thankful whoever is shooting always shoots off-center and to the right. These guys must not be professionals. My dad aims his gun and fires. I hear a man yelp as I realize my dad's shot has made impact.

I grab onto Skylar's arm and almost pull her as I try to increase our speed across the creek. With our next step, I suddenly feel Skylar lose her footing and begin to fall. I keep the grip on her arm and pull her back to her feet, but not before she partially submerges under the water. The fear sweeping across her face is immense and I assure her, "I told you I had you. I won't let you go under."

The water pressure picks up, and I begin to doubt myself.

We have only a few more yards, and I know that I have to do everything I can to be strong and stable enough for both of us. I hear her fearful breathing over the sound of the water rushing into us. More gunfire is exchanged. My body ignites with the promise I made to her that I would protect her. I feel pain pierce my torso as my ribs begin to ache and get uncomfortable again. I realize though, that no matter the circumstances of our relationship, I won't let her down. I can't let her down.

I become a solid rock as I pave the way towards the edge of the creek bed. I see my dad aim and shoot multiple times as we approach. I hear another painful cry as my dad's shot makes contact again. We reach the edge, and before Skylar can climb out of the creek, I let go of her grip and pick her up around the waist and set her next to my dad.

I see that her pants and part of her torso are soaked with creek water as I lift her out. I quickly get out of the water, and my dad says, "C'mon, this way."

Behind me, the men aren't entering the water. My stomach sinks as I come to the realization that we probably shouldn't have either. I keep my revelation to myself, as I don't want to slow down our escape route, especially considering the immense contact Skylar had with the water. I feel a pit in my stomach forming as failure sweeps over me. I wonder if I'll ever be able to keep my promise of protection to her.

We make our way quickly into the trees and up the steep incline of the hill. We're forced to grab onto tree trunks in order to pull ourselves up. When we reach the top, I turn back to see the men cowering at the same spot I last saw them. I say quietly, "I don't think they're coming across." My dad turns to look, and when I see his facial expression change I think he's come to the same realization about the water that I have.

"All right, now is our chance. We have to keep moving, put some distance between us."

He motions for us as he takes off at a jog. I let Skylar fill the gap between me and him as I place myself to our rear. The pain in my head begins to intensify with each step. My ribs continue to throb—the pain reliever I took hours ago is wearing off. A few minutes pass of a steady jog, and I become light-headed and nauseous. I struggle to say, "Hold on," as I begin to collapse. I brace myself on a nearby tree and slump to the ground.

Skylar reaches me first.

Concerned, she asks, "What's wrong?" As she becomes more attentive, I hear her say, "Max, what happened? You're bleeding."

I look up at her, confused, and mutter, "I am?"

CHAPTER EIGHTEEN

MAX: Sunday, May 24

My dad reaches us and says, "Whoa, buddy!" as he reaches to my side.

I look down as he prods at my side and see blood soaking through my shirt. I struggle to lift my shirt as my dad analyzes my condition. My head becomes fuzzy again, so I decide to just let my dad do his examination.

"I think that Vicodin wore off. My head and ribs are aching again. Did you bring it?"

My dad responds, "Yeah we did. But I think I should get this bullet out first."

Skylar and I both say simultaneously, "Bullet?"

"Both of you just calm down. Seems as though you caught a bullet back at the creek. Does this hurt?"

I wince as my dad prods deeper into the wound. "Um, yeah, obviously. How about I shoot you and poke it like that and then ask if it hurts?"

"Max, I can see the bullet. The wound isn't very deep. If I had a knife, I could probably pry it out and then bandage you up. It'll take the pressure off if we can get it out."

I glare at him, and as much as I want to just get up and continue on, I say, "There's a pocket knife in my backpack. Front compartment in the bottom."

My dad looks at Skylar and says, "Sky?"

"Yeah—yeah sorry, I'll grab it."

At this point, I've already wiggled my arm out of the side strap so that my backpack casually hangs on my opposite side. Skylar kneels down to open it, and I remember her soaked clothes. "Did you bring spare clothes?" I ask her.

"Yeah, I have a couple of extra things."

"You should change while he's doing this and set your clothes over there to dry out," I say as I point to an opening in the tree coverage letting light in. "You'll probably get uncomfortable if you don't," I add.

She hands my dad the knife and responds, "Yeah, I guess I could do that. Are you sure though? I can help."

I look at my dad and try to telepathically tell him to confirm. "We'll be fine," he says.

"Okay, I'll be quick. Be right back."

"Don't go too far, Sky, and keep an ear out for anything or anyone."

She walks a few feet away and hides behind a few trees. As she walks over, she takes her backpack off her shoulders and starts unzipping it. When she's farther than earshot distance I say to my dad, "She was covered from the chest down in that water."

"Yeah, and you have an open wound and were in it. I don't think you got any water contact up here, just looks like your legs." He looks me in the eyes and says, "You're probably going to feel a little pinch."

I feel him place the knife against my side and grit my teeth as I anticipate the incision. I try to take my mind off of the pain and ask, "Do you think that's why those men didn't cross into the water? Because of the contamination?"

As he slices into my flesh he says sarcastically, "I'd like to just believe that maybe they couldn't swim."

The pain isn't nearly as bad as I'd expected. Maybe because my ribs were already hurting and my head pounding. I feel a deeper incision being made as I see Skylar reappear from the trees in a different outfit. This time she's wearing a pair of dark cut-off jean shorts and a black t-shirt. I can see the straps of her burnt-red sports bra poking out of the top of the V-neck area. Really, though, she would probably look smokin' hot in a brown paper sack.

She walks over to place her soaked clothing in the sun like I had suggested and then walks back to my side.

"I don't have any other shoes, I'll just have to hope these dry out soon." I look down at her soggy Chuck Taylors. She grabs my free hand with both of her hands as she kneels beside me. "Doing okay?"

I reply, "Considering the circumstances, yeah."

My dad warns, "One more and we'll be in the clear, okay?"

I feel the knife dig into my side, and instinctively I grip her hand harder. I nearly pull her down and immediately feel apologetic. I mutter, "Sorry." And she gives me a sweet smile in return as I release her hand.

I feel the pressure from my side release, and my dad says, "Here it is, looks like a 9mm hollow point."

I look in his hand to see the bloody bullet. "We should hurry. Let's bandage this thing up. Where's that Vicodin?"

My dad takes the backpack off of his back and brings it to his lap to unzip it. He pulls out the first-aid kit and a bottle of water. He hands me the water and opens the first-aid kit. The vial of Vicodin is inside. He takes two into his hand and then breaks one in half. He hands me a full tablet and half of the other and says, "Here. I'm not sure you're ready for two yet but I can imagine you need more than one." He puts the other half back inside the vial and places it into a compartment in the kit.

"Thanks."

I pop the pills in my mouth and take a healthy swig of the water. I swallow the pills and realize I was a bit thirstier than I had imagined so I drink nearly the rest of the bottle. My head immediately begins to lose its epic fuzziness.

My dad takes a few things out of the first-aid kit and starts working on bandaging up my side. "I should probably stitch you up, but I don't know how much time we have. I'm just going to patch you up as well as I can until we can get to safer turf."

"That's fine," I reply. "I wouldn't mind moving on anyways. I don't feel right being out here like this, so close to what just happened."

I turn to Skylar and ask, "You okay?"

Her response pegs as oddly defensive. "Um, yeah, why?"

"Just making sure, that's all. How's your face?"

"My face is just fine, Max, thanks for asking," she says sarcastically.

"I didn't mean anything by it, I was just going to say you could take the other half of that Vicodin if it was bothering you."

"Oh—well, no I'm fine. Thanks, though."

My dad chimes in. "See, you two defused that quickly. Making progress."

We both glare at him, and he replies, "Hey! I'm just saying! You two argue like an old grouchy married couple."

She stands up and walks over to check on her clothes as my dad finishes doctoring up my side. He puts a final piece of gauze on and says, "There, that should hold ya over for a little while."

He starts to put the supplies back in the first-aid kit, and I can't help but ask, "Dad, where did you learn to do this? I mean all the medical stuff. Every time someone gets hurt you seem to know what to do."

"Well, Max, it was either going to be engineering or medical, and even though I chose the former, I still wanted to know a little bit about the latter."

I'm a little taken back by his response because I didn't know that he had an interest in the medical field. My mom had taken a few courses for nursing but never followed through with it because she wanted to be a teacher instead—even though the pay was horrible.

He stands up and slings his backpack across his shoulder and then extends an arm to assist me in standing. He asks, "How are you feeling?"

"Better, I think my body was just out of whack from the pain and being a little dehydrated. I actually feel a lot better now."

"Good, we should probably start heading east again. Let's get our guns reloaded and make sure we've got all of our stuff."

Skylar walks back toward us, and my dad begins to fill her in on the generic plan we made. He asks about her clothes, and she says that they're dry enough to put in her backpack. I suggest that we take the food out of her backpack and put in mine, just so we don't risk things getting wet and ruined.

I really just suggested it because I have no idea how contaminated that water was, and I don't want to risk poisoning us. So far, she's shown no sign of contagion, although we have no idea what the beginning stages look like.

I can't help but wonder how these people became infected. Is this airborne? Are we far enough out of the city that there isn't a public water supply anymore? Why haven't we seen any other people like us? I took a shower in the water, what, like Friday? Why haven't I changed yet? I wonder if it hurts when the process, the change, the...whatever happens.

We walk for what seems like forever. It's really only been a couple of hours. We haven't really talked much, just the occasional "Hey, let's stop for a snack" or "Hey, I need to pee" type stuff. We did have a laugh though on our last bathroom break. Skylar mentioned that in all the apocalypse shows, she's never really noticed any of them stopping for the bathroom.

"I mean really, though, how are we supposed to believe that it's real if they don't even have to take a leak?"

"Well, maybe they're dehydrated. It's not like they're eating as gourmet as we are."

"No, really, I've peed in the woods more times than I'm proud to admit on this trip."

My dad says, "Well, I guess we keep it real then."

We all laugh.

Skylar notices the buildings in the distance first. She points, and when my eyes finally focus, I make out what appears to be a large farm. There are two large silos surrounded by a few various sized buildings.

I say, "Let's get as close as possible and then check things out from a distance first."

"Yeah, let's head to the furthest side of this tree line," Skylar says as she points to the trees closest to the buildings.

We jog along the edge of the trees and slow down as we

reach the end. We hold back and post up to assess our surroundings. About five minutes go by, and nothing happens. We make note that there are numerous farming machines around the property that we may be able to utilize.

I tell them, "Let's focus on getting a decent set of wheels before we do anything else."

"Looks like the opening for this building is probably on that side," Dad says, as he points to the east side of the garage. "We'll head there and check things out on the way. Stay aware, okay?"

We take off in our regular formation towards the building. When we reach the building, we stop to properly survey the other side, one at a time. My dad motions that the coast is clear and we head over with him.

The building is large and open. The outside is painted a typical barn-crimson-red with white trim. The roof appears to be recently replaced, with its matching white tin. The side we're on has one large door for machinery and a small door for human entry. On the sides of the building are small windows with white trim lining them. This building is the largest of the three with the other two appearing to be the same design, their only difference being size.

The main door to the building is open, exposing the farm machinery left unattended inside. We look around carefully as we examine the contents of the building. I spot a couple different sized tractors and a combine harvester. The smaller tractor has an uncovered seat, while the larger has an enclosed area around it. The harvester is easily larger than the biggest tractor with its extravagant harvesting attachment on the front.

Near the far side of the building is a small bench with miscellaneous trinkets sprawled out. A little black box sits in the furthest corner. I walk over and pull the little box to the edge of the table. I open it and find a key ring with one key on it. I quickly grab it up in hopes that it starts one of these units. I rush back to my dad and show him the key.

I ask, "Would you like to do the honors?"

He replies, "Just one? Oh man, I hope it's the harvester, that thing looks like it could plow through any terrain."

"I just hope it starts one of the three or we'll have to check all the barns for whatever it starts. Our luck, it's a small riding mower."

"Hey, our luck hasn't been too horrible, we're still here, considering," he says.

The mood changes and I reply, "Well, not all of us."

I'm reminded of how much I failed when I let Wiley get captured. I have to find a way to get back there and get him back. I'll forever hold myself responsible unless I do something.

My dad hops onto the harvester and opens the glass door. He takes the key and puts it in the ignition. A second goes by, and he pulls his arm out of the machine and says, "Not a winner."

"Here," he says as he tosses the key to me. "Try that one."

I hop onto the side of the smallest tractor next to the harvester and try my luck on the ignition. The key slides in but takes no effect when I attempt to turn it over.

I climb out and say, "No luck here, either."

I look at Skylar and say, "Here, catch." She catches the key and I tell her, "Make this one count." She grabs onto the handle on the side of the tractor and pulls herself up. I always forget how small she is until she's forced to do something to test her size. She was barely able to hike her leg up to even climb onto the side of the tractor.

She opens the hatch of the door on the tractor and climbs inside. She looks like a child sitting inside this big foreign thing. I see her slide the key into the ignition. She looks over at me hanging off of the small tractor so I give her a hopeful smile. She turns the key and I hear the engine sputter to life.

She cheers, "Yes!" And I hop off the small tractor to rush over to her.

"Good job. Looks like you've got better luck than we do!"

My dad meets us and says, "Good score, Sky! Let's shut her down and clear this crap out of our way."

Skylar turns the engine off and climbs out of the seated compartment. Instead of letting her jump down I say, "Here," and hold my arms out. She comes closer to me and puts her hands on my shoulders to stabilize. I put my hands on her waist and lift her off the tractor with ease and onto the ground. I set her down in front of me. Her hands remain on my shoulders and mine on her waist as we make eye contact.

She whispers, "Thanks."

And even though I didn't have words to say back, my dad interrupts by saying, "Hey, a little help over here."

She takes her hands off my shoulders and gives a small smile as she turns to walk over to my dad. He's trying to move a snow removal attachment that belongs to one of these tractors. We all grab a side and are able to move it far enough out of the way to clear our path. We look outside of the barn just to verify we had a clear path outside, too. I hadn't noticed a house in the distance up the gravel driveway until now. Or the person just right outside of it walking towards us.

I point that direction and say, "Time to go; we've got company."

We rush back over to the tractor, and my dad climbs into the driver's seat. The unit was only made for one person but the seat is large enough that Skylar can sit on the inside of the cab, too. I help her climb up and follow behind her. I hold onto the handle on the side and put a firm footing on the step.

My dad turns the ignition and the engine sputters but

doesn't start. I see the person from the distance begin to close the gap between us. My heart begins to pound as I reach back with my free hand and take my gun from the holster. My dad turns over the ignition, and the engine sputters again. I see the person pick up their pace and tell my dad, "Get this thing moving."

Skylar reaches across and says, "Let me try." She places her hand on the key and gently turns over the ignition. The engine sputters for a split second and then roars to life again.

My dad half laughs and says, "Maybe you should drive this thing, too."

Urgency lining my voice I say, "Well it would be nice if someone would drive it and get us out of this damn barn."

My dad puts the engine in drive and pushes his hand down on the accelerator next to the steering wheel. We make our way out of the barn as the person gains ground on us. The ravaged look on the man's face tells me that he was out for blood, not for his tractor.

We pull away just as the man leaps towards us. He grasps onto the back of the tractor, and as he tries to gain entry, he loses grip and falls onto the ground. I turn to look as he growls and screams towards us. He pulls himself off of the ground and begins to sprint towards us. The tractor roars to life, and the increased speed puts a distance between the man and us. I continue to look back, his deranged body getting smaller as we get further away.

CHAPTER NINETEEN

MAX: Sunday, May 24

I feel comfortable enough to holster my gun and relax for a moment.

The breeze is a nice reminder that I'm still alive, that I'm still me. Well, the me I am now, after everything that's happened. I'll never be *me* again.

There is nothing surrounding us, and I'm completely okay with that. There are trees and empty crop fields. I really don't know where we are, but I know we're probably going the right direction. I really don't know what the hell we're going to do when we get to the cabin, either, but I guess we'll take this one thing at a time.

Right now, the plan is to just get there. We haven't been there in a while, the cabin. My dad and I stopped going as much when we lost Mom. He still goes there without me, but I just haven't been able to bring myself to go with him.

I feel a bump and look up. I see that we're closing in on a

patch of wooded area. I look inside the cab and see my dad easing up on the throttle.

He sarcastically says, "Just a bit of turbulence."

Over the sound of the engine and the small brush crunching beneath our wheels, I hear a person. I look to my left and see a group of maybe half a dozen people. Then I see him, the man they're chasing.

"Help me!" he screams.

Fear sweeps across his face, and I yell to my dad, "Stop, we have to help him." I jump off the side of the tractor and pull out my gun.

Before I can get a shot off, one of the deranged women leaps forward and tackles the man. His screams pierce through me as I begin to shoot. Two other deranged begin kicking the man violently. His screams stop, and the only sound I hear is the constant thudding of their feet against his lifeless body.

"Max, come on, now, we've got to go," my dad urges.

I fire two more shots and take one of them down. I climb back onto the tractor and away we go. It turns my stomach to realize this is the world we live in now.

After we're in the clear, my dad lets Skylar operate the tractor for a few miles. She giggles as she plows over the terrain. I reload our guns and go back to investigation mode, checking out the sights but also keeping an eye out for any dangers, like the herd of people we stumbled upon. I constantly have to shake the memory of the sounds the man made as he was beaten to death.

In the distance, I see two silos and think for a second that I'm having déjà vu. When we get closer, I see that the building has a large tank next to the barn. Bold letters on the side read: PROPANE. I was hoping it would have been diesel to fuel up our tractor. When get even closer we see that there are numerous small machines around the property: small tractors, lawnmowers, etc.

I lean toward the inside of the tractor and say, "We should probably fuel up. There might be gas cans somewhere over there. I haven't seen any movement. Go ahead and pull up to that barn entrance."

I point ahead to the larger of the two barns. By the exterior looks of this place, it probably wasn't as successful of a farm as the last one we visited. The building's paint is partially chipped away, and the roof has shingles missing. There is a small house about two hundred feet from the barn that looks run down.

I imagine the owner of this property to be a shotgun-toting old man who lost his wife years ago. Perhaps she was the one keeping order to the property, and now that she's gone, things have gone downhill.

My mind flashes back to after my mother died—when my dad couldn't keep up with things around the house. Laundry piled up, dishes cluttered the countertops, he wouldn't get out of his sweatpants for days. Wiley had come over nearly every day to help—bringing take-out and cleaning, dragging my dad outside for fresh air. Then, finally, about two months later he somehow just snapped out of it and got back to reality.

Even though I was young, I still recognized the pain my dad went through when he lost my mom. He would act so strong one moment, and then break down the next. I think he finally just became numb to the pain and decided to get on with his life, that she wouldn't want him to dwell.

We pull up next to the barn and shut the engine off. I hop down first and turn around to assist Skylar. Without exchanging words, she places her hands on my shoulders as I place my hands on her small waist. I don't allow things to become awkward so I let go of her as soon as I've lifted her off the tractor and onto the ground. She mutters, "Thanks," as I turn away.

I start looking around the outside of the barn. There's an old lawn mower next to the door but no fuel can. I walk past the mower and try to open the door to the barn. I fumble with the handle, but the door is locked. My dad jumps to the ground.

"Any luck?"

"No. This door is locked. We can check that other barn though."

"Or if we find a hose, we can siphon from the mower to the tractor." He points to the old lawn mower I just walked by.

"There's one of those roll-up garden hose things on the side of the house up there. Want me to go grab the hose off of it?" Skylar says.

"Yeah, good eye, Sky. I'll run over to the other barn and see if I can get in there."

"I'll get things ready here," I add.

Skylar takes off jogging in the direction of the house as I turn around to make sure there is fuel in the lawnmower. I take the cap off of the fuel tank and give the mower a firm shake. The sound of fuel sloshes and I smile, a bit pleased with myself, and turn back to the tractor to access the fuel reservoir.

As I open the compartment where the fuel tank is, the sound of scuffling footsteps catches me off guard. I turn towards the barn where my dad had headed to see if the noise was coming from him but see nothing. My heart drops when my mind goes to Skylar.

I turn back to the direction of the house, and my fears are brought to life when I see a man practically dragging Skylar with his hand over her mouth. She's flailing her legs and trying to pry his hand off of her. My mind flashes to the memory of the guard taking her hostage, and I hate myself for letting her get into danger again.

I start to move towards him, and a person startles me from around the side of the barn and orders, "Don't move, kid."

This man appears to be slightly smaller than the other and is in his mid-thirties. One hand holds a handgun pointed at me, and the other, the hose that Skylar went to retrieve. I turn to look back at Skylar, and the man's voice hardens and says, "Son, do you have a death wish?"

I hear more movement and see my dad appear behind him with his gun raised.

He says, "Do *you*?"

I begin to feel a bit of hope in this epically shitty situation.

My dad insists, "Let the girl go, buddy. And then be on your way."

A third younger voice appears from behind my dad and says, "Clever one, old man. Now drop your gun." From the looks of the three men, I either assume they are brothers, or the youngest boy is one of their sons.

My dad lowers his gun and drops it to the ground. The youngest of the three says, "Now kick it over here."

He does as he says and kicks his gun towards the boy. I say a silent prayer that they can't see mine hiding under my shirt.

The boy appears to be high school-aged but a couple years younger than me. He looks dirty, and his clothes are tattered. I can't help but wonder what they have gone through since the world started falling apart.

I speak up. "What do you want?"

The guy that has Skylar captive says, "Run out of fuel? How about you take the hose and siphon the fuel like you had planned?"

"And then what?"

"Then we're going to tie you up and let you sit in the barn until you don't hear us anymore, after we take the tractor."

I sarcastically say, "Well, the barn's locked, so you'll have to make another plan."

"Good thing I have the key, hotshot." I sense that he's lying, but I don't have the time to read his poker face.

My dad urges to me, "Just do it, Max."

I don't want to do what they want, but the fear of not knowing what they will do to Skylar drives me to take the hose out of the guy's hands. He takes his now-free hand and places it under his weapon to steady his grip. I give him a hesitant look of dissatisfaction. The man holding Skylar becomes impatient and drives the side of his gun into her rib cage.

My blood begins to boil as she groans under the grip of his hand around her mouth.

"Boy, you need to hurry up," he asserts.

I take the hose and put one end inside of the lawnmower. I stretch the rest of the hose out and walk towards the tractor. As I get to the tractor, I look back at my dad; he nods his head in approval so I take the hose in my mouth and begin sucking air through. After a few solid attempts, I'm caught off guard by the fuel filling my mouth. I try to spit and hack it up as I push the hose into the tank of the tractor.

The fuel flows into the tank, and the man satisfyingly says, "Atta boy."

I wipe my mouth on my arm multiple times and wipe the inside of the mouth with the sleeve of my shirt. The men begin to laugh, and when I look up at them, I see another man walking towards us. I say, "Oh, is your friend late to the party?"

They give me confused looks and turn around to see what I'm talking about. Just as they do, the fourth man takes off into a sprint towards Skylar and the oldest guy. Before he can react, the man leaps towards him and knocks him off balance. He falls to the ground and pins Skylar under him. I hear the impact as they both hit the ground.

The deranged man begins beating the man as he tries to turn around. Skylar pulls with all of her might to free herself as I run towards her. I grab ahold of her as soon as the man begins to stand up and pull her towards me. The man fights to find his gun as he stands up and gets another furious punch to the torso. He winces and by the time he can react, one of the other men shoots the deranged man.

My dad runs over to help us off the ground. The two younger men reach us at the same time, with weapons drawn. The youngest boy pulls the hose out of the tractor as he walks by and secures the cap.

As I turn to look at the men, the oldest grabs Skylar again and says to us, "Back away."

"No," I reply.

He shoves the gun into her side again, and as she winces he says, "The faster you back away, the faster we'll get on our way."

I interrupt him and say, "You're not taking her."

"Ain't no purpose in taking her, boy. Soon as y'all get moving to the other side of that barn, we'll load up and let her go."

"Why should I believe you?"

"What other choice do you have?"

CHAPTER TWENTY

MAX: Sunday, May 24

My dad grabs my arm and begins to pull me backward. I stumble as he pulls me farther away. The men start throwing their backpacks into the tractor, and the two younger men climb inside.

"Farther, boys," he insists as he backs himself closer to the tractor.

One of the men says loudly, "We've got company closing in. Time to come on, Don."

I look past them and see another figure moving quickly towards us. The engine of the tractor sputters and then comes to life. In one swift motion, Don releases his grip around Skylar to grab onto the handle on the side of the tractor to pull himself up.

He takes his leg, rears up, and kicks her straight in the back throwing her towards us. She falls to the ground forcefully as I run towards her. She's able to stand up unsteadily and half run/crawl in my direction. I get to her quickly and help her to her feet.

She's covered in dirt and grass from head to toe, and her face is tearstained. She practically leaps into my arms as the tractor hurriedly gets away. I hear the man hanging off the tractor yell, "Listen here boys, this is a dog-eat-dog type world we're living in now. Sorry to have to do this, but it's either you, or us. And well, you know what we pick."

I try to put my arms around Skylar to keep her from collapsing but see the immediate threat approaching us. I push her to my left, under my arm and pull my gun out of its holstered position. With one shot, the growling person hits the ground.

By now the tractor is too far to accurately shoot, plus it wouldn't be productive for either of us to have a damaged tractor or a deadly firefight. As much as I'm pissed at what they've done, I don't go after them. I just put my arms back around Skylar and pull her back onto her feet.

My dad's voice comes from behind me. "A little help?"

I turn around and see he's being attacked by a petite woman. She throws a vicious punch towards him but misses and loses balance. As she falls to the ground, she leaps towards him and attempts to grab onto his leg. He kicks her fiercely in the head and knocks her back slightly. I raise my gun and aim for her momentarily still body, and with a single pull of the trigger, she's gone.

My dad says in an irritated tone, "Have either of you seen my damn gun? Those a-holes took it, didn't they? I loved that thing."

Skylar reaches for her gun and says quietly, "Here, just take mine. I'm not very good with it anyways."

I interrupt her from handing it to him when I see the dull black of his gun sticking out from some grass. "That dumbass kid must have forgotten to pick it up after you kicked it to him," I say, half laughing.

Skylar repositions her partially drawn weapon back into its holstered position. I feel the pain of my torso begin to take over my thoughts again, and as I reach down to hold my side, I see fresh blood covering my shirt.

"You okay, buddy?"

"Yeah, I'm fine," I say as I take my hand off of my side so I don't appear as weak as I feel.

"When we get to the next safe place, I'll redress your bandages. But, let's focus on getting somewhere first."

Skylar speaks up. "Which direction are we going?"

My dad points and says, "We'll continue southeast until we're about to run out of daylight. Unless we find something we just can't pass up on."

"No more splitting up. That could have been a lot worse back there," I say.

"Yeah, we let our guard down too much there," my dad replies. It's not just the deranged we have to be worried about, it's the survivors, too."

We've been walking for at least an hour now, making sure to be cautious with our surroundings. We haven't come into contact with any survivors, but we've seen a few deranged. Luckily, we saw them before they could realize we were there, and got away without a confrontation.

We had to cross a small creek about a half-hour ago. My dad and I were able to hop across with ease, but Skylar ended up soaking one of her feet when she tried to jump across.

Another example of an advantage of being tall and a disadvantage of being short.

She tried her best to follow our lead and jump across, but her short little legs just didn't cooperate. The look on her face was priceless when she failed, like a small child who fails at something they see adults do. My dad and I both laughed until she finally cracked a smile, and for the first time in a long while, the mood was light again.

Skylar asks, "What time is it?"

I look at my watch and reply, "A little after seven."

"Any chance of stopping soon? I'm pretty hungry and tired."

My dad says, "Let's try for just a little bit longer, maybe a half-hour. Here, let me grab something for you."

"Thanks, Keith."

He reaches back and grabs a granola bar from his backpack's side compartment and hands it to her. She opens the wrapper and starts eating it. With a partially full mouth she mumbles, "Hey, is that a park?"

"I thought we might be going this way," says my dad in a satisfied tone. "We should be able to make our way closer and check things out. There should be a bait shop with some more food and drinks. And we should be able to find somewhere to camp for the night."

"Wait, is this that place you took me as a kid to fish?"

He smiles at me. "Yep."

I was young, but I remember coming here. We would rent a boat and take it out to fish. My mom would pack our cooler full of snacks, and we would spend the day out on the lake. We used to dock at this little hidden island and eat our lunch at the one lone picnic table.

"Dad, think we could go to the island?"

Skylar looks at my confused, "What island?"

"In the middle of the lake, there's a small piece of land that I used to take Max out to when we went fishing. We would dock over there and eat our lunch. We'd climb trees, throw rocks, swim off the island...we've had a lot of memories on this lake." He half-smiles in my direction.

"An island? Sounds pretty secure to me, I vote we camp there tonight," she says.

"We could clear that island in no time, Dad, and set up camp. My vote's there, too."

"We don't even know if there will be a boat available, let alone one we could start. One step at a time." He hesitates for a second and says, "But if it's an option, we'll do it. But, really, don't get your hopes up."

He's right. I shouldn't get my hopes up. I'm holding on to the memory of normalcy so tight that I know I'll be let down if something disallows it from happening. Thinking about being out on that island brings me a type of peace I didn't know existed in this currently fucked up world.

We approach the park's fence with caution. The fence is wooden and frames the perimeter of the property. I assume it's for aesthetic purposes, considering it provides no actual ability to stop anything. My dad and I are too tall to fit through the middle rungs, so we both hike our legs up and sideways hop over. Skylar is able to easily duck and crouch through the middle with ease. With every step, we are vigilant to not bring attention to ourselves.

We walk past a few rows of trees until we see the houses that line the pavement ahead. We stop for a minute and listen. We hear nothing other than the sound of nature inviting us in.

"We must have missed the evacuation when you bumped your head and left us for a while."

"You act like I intentionally stayed unconscious, Dad."

"I know, I know, I'm just saying, the lack of people is so eerie."

With a tight formation and drawn guns, we make our way

behind the row of houses, past the playground, towards the bait shop. With every step, I hear Skylar's uneasy breathing. I don't think she'll ever quite get used to the concept of being stealthy.

Fortunately, the park isn't very large, so we reach the bait shop fairly quickly. I put my gun away as we walk up the handicap accessible ramp to the overhang of the shop. The bait shop has a wooden walkway three-quarters of the way around with an entry door on one side and a flap opening on the main side. I remember back to when I was a child—I could barely see over the counter that was always piled with different snacks and bait supplies. Now, I almost hit my head on the overhang.

Skylar leans over the railing looking towards the lake. She turns around and catches me looking at her. I quickly turn my head back to the bait shop and begin surveying it more. My dad is busy wiggling the handle of the door and trying to use a stick to pry the door open. I walk over to see how he is doing and spy a deadbolt.

"Dad, no amount of prying is going to bypass that lock."

"You got an idea then?" he says as he looks up at me.

"What about the part of the awning that opens on the side? I bet it has hooks holding it from the inside. A little prying and I bet we can pop it open."

He stops fiddling with the door and stands up. We walk over by the awning where Skylar is standing. I grab onto the awning and pull. Something is holding it securely but feels uneasy. I tell the two of them, "Grab some sturdy sticks and shove them into the opening when I pull on this. That should give us the leverage we need."

They both quickly walk down the ramp and grab a few sticks each. I pull the awning back open as far as I can and they push two sticks each into the opening.

I reach over with one hand and secure Skylar's sticks in place.

I tell them, "Alright, one...two...pull!" And just like that, with one solid burst, the awning pops open. In all of my excitement over our success, I hadn't noticed that Skylar fell. She must have pulled so hard that she lost balance and fell backward.

She's sitting on the downhill of the ramp on the other side, wiping dirt and debris off of her. I quickly walk over and extend my hand for support to help her up. She places her hand in mine, and I pull her off the ground. She immediately pulls her hand away, and while at first, I assume she's trying to keep her distance, I see the bloody streaks she left in my hand.

I immediately say, "Are you okay?"

"Yeah," she says quietly as she examines her hand.

"Let me see it."

"I'm fine, Max."

"Skylar," I insist.

She rolls her eyes and places her hand palm up in the air for me to take as she looks away. I bring it closer to examine and see that she has several splinters lodged in her hand among a lot of scraped skin along her palm and wrist.

"How about you two lovebirds come over here?"

"How about you come over here? And bring your backpack," I reply with angst.

He walks over without hesitation and right away sees Skylar's mangled hand.

"Ouch," he says.

"It's really not that bad. Can I just have a bandage from the first-aid kit?"

"Don't be that stubborn, Sky, let me take a look."

I let my dad take her hand as she lets out an exaggerated sigh. He shimmies his backpack off and says, "Grab the tweezers out of the first-aid kit."

I hurriedly kneel and unzip the backpack, locate the first-aid kit, and open it up. I fumble around to find the tweezers and hand them to him. I go back to the kit and continue to grab some wound compresses, gauze, and adhesive wrap. She takes a deep breath as he pulls the first splinter out, a huge chunk of wood that he flicks off of the tweezers.

He says, "All right Sky, I see two more big ones. Probably close your eyes or look away."

She reaches over and grabs onto my hand with her free hand. She squeezes tight in anticipation of the next splinter. Without hesitating, he shakes the tweezers empty and goes in for the next big piece. She grips my hand tighter as I watch my dad do his work.

"Okay, just a few smaller splinters. I'm going to do them one after another."

"Okay," she mutters. She loosens the grip on my hand and then releases me, giving me a tender and thankful half-smile. It reminds me of when she held my hand while my dad removed the bullet from my side, just the thought of it makes my body ache.

"Grab a bottle of water, Max."

My dad takes the bottle and rinses her hand as gently as possible. He then asks for the supplies and dresses her hand. "You two really need to stop getting hurt. We're going to have to get a new first-aid kit pretty soon." I humor him with a slight chuckle.

I hear footsteps bordering us and turn towards them with my gun already drawn. I point it in the direction of the sound, and more indistinct shuffling follows. I begin to panic.

I tell them faintly, "Back up closer to the bait shop."

CHAPTER TWENTY-ONE

MAX: Sunday, May 24

Before I can take another step, I see a beautiful doe and her fawn gingerly stroll by.

I let out a sigh of relief and lower my gun. "It was just a deer."

My dad finishes bandaging Skylar's hand and tosses the supplies back inside the backpack. The sun has started setting, and we are losing daylight fast. Skylar says, "There's a few boats docked over there."

Past the railing Skylar had been leaned over are two 20'-30' boats and a few small rental boats. I'm almost certain we can get one of the rentals, but it would be really nice to take one of the bigger boats.

We walk back over to the awning, and my dad nods at the opening to indicate he wants me to hop inside first. I peek my head inside the dimly lit bait shop and grab onto the side to pull myself up and over. My landing isn't even close to graceful, and I end up making more noise than I expect.

I quickly reach over and unlock the door allowing them entry. When I turn around to check out our score, I almost lose it.

A person, an old lady, is lying on the ground in the back of the bait shop.

At first, I assume she's dead but after staring attentively at her, I realize she has shallow inconsistent breaths. A row of keyrings hangs above the woman.

I whisper to Skylar and my dad, "Grab whatever you can find. I'm going for those keys."

I start slowly inching my way towards her. I hear them behind me, shoving random shit into their backpacks. The woman hasn't moved but continues to take a breath every now and then.

She looks like she may be in her mid-60s, with short, mostly gray hair. She's dainty, about the size of Skylar, but not as feminine. I watch her breathing as I continue to make my way towards the keys. As I get closer, I see that there are numerous single keys, and then three larger keys on bigger chains. I pretty much assume that one of those three should start at least one of the two larger boats sitting just outside.

I'm going to get those keys, and I'm going to figure out which boat we'll be taking tonight.

I can't help but think that she may be a dormant deranged person, but then I remember the public service announcement about the comatose type people. They didn't go into detail on the characteristics, so I don't know what to expect, or if that was even true. I'm standing within a few inches of her as I try to use my height to allow me to reach over her to access the keys. But as I reach, my balance fails me and my footing slips slightly.

I accidentally touch her with my foot.

I hold my breath and freeze as I look down to determine if I've disturbed her. After a few seconds, she doesn't show any signs of movement, so I quickly pick each of the larger keys off the hooks and place them in my jean pocket.

I turn around to walk away, and the woman lets out a faint sigh. I slowly turn back around and stare at her for what seems like eternity until my dad says, "Max, she's gone, c'mon." I instantly feel guilty that my accidental contact may have just killed this feeble old woman. He grabs my arm and reiterates in a more solid tone, "Max, come on."

I turn away from the newly deceased woman and see that Skylar and my dad have both filled their backpacks and are holding rolled-up sleeping bags. Skylar picks one up off of the ground and hands it to me. I shove my arm through the middle to get a better grip and still have access to my hand.

I tap my pocket. "I've got three keys, and I assume one of them will start one of those boats. We ready?"

Before they can respond, commotion from outside alerts us. As I scan around us trying to find the culprit, I think back to the deer and hope it's just them. There, in the short distance, I see people moving toward us. From their rhythm, I assume they aren't in their right mind. I count four bodies moving quickly toward us and say, "We've got to go, now."

At first, we try to slowly and quietly make our way out of the bait shop, but we soon realize the deranged know of our presence. They begin to move quickly as we pick up our pace. We hop over the railing of the bait shop and start running to the pier. The sun has mostly gone down, and the visibility is in that in-between stage of dusk. I reach into my pocket and pull out the three keys.

I hand my dad two of them and say, "Go to the furthest boat, I'm going to this one," as I nod towards the closest boat. "Chances are one or both of them will start. If it's mine, you'll be far enough away to pull your guns and take anyone out before I can get the boat to you. If it's yours...I'll get there, don't worry. Take Skylar with you."

We reach the pier, and they take off running to the furthest boat. I quickly hop inside the nearest and into the driver's seat. As fast as I can, I take the key and move it toward the ignition.

I drop it.

"Seriously?" I say under my breath and think, *Are you f'n kidding me, dude.*

I immediately pick the key off the ground and slam it into the ignition, turn it over—and nothing. Failure hits me hard, and as I look up, I see that the deranged have reached the pier. I grab the key out of the ignition and slide it back into the safety of my pocket.

My heart jumps; I need to get out of here. A man, medium build, middle-aged – reaches my boat first. He grabs onto the handle and pulls himself on board. A low growl escapes his vocal cords as he sets his eyes on me. A smaller, younger male boards the boat following him.

I'm trying to quickly decide my best escape route, and I notice a smaller rental boat beside us. I make my way backward, slowly, to the furthest end of my boat which will allow adequate space for a successful jump. Using the metal railing of the boat's roof, I pull myself up and into position.

I wait.

I stand there watching as they continue to board the boat in pursuit of me. Before the last of the four boards, the closest one grows impatient and leaps towards me. I simultaneously leap from the side and land onto the smaller boat. Reluctantly, my sleeping bag absorbs most of the impact.

I quickly get to my feet and see the last of the four, who wasn't able to board the boat, making her way towards me. She appears to be a young woman, mid-twenties, dark brown hair, and a heavier build. Her face expresses such hatred and aggression. I look back and see the other three stumbling into each other, unable to make their way off of the boat. I plant my feet firmly so I don't lose balance while the boat rocks back and forth.

I wait for the woman to make her move before I make mine.

She leaps forward, and I jump at the same time. I land on the boat beside me and without hesitation bring myself back onto my feet. I scramble back onto the dock and run as fast as I can to the boat at the end. Within a second, I notice that I don't hear the boat running and I instantly feel like our plan has failed.

I jump onto the boat, and Skylar says, "Max, neither key worked," in a panicked voice. I run past her and pull the key out of my pocket. With one swift move, I force the key into the ignition and turn.

The boat roars to life and relief overtakes me.

My dad hastily hangs out of the boat and unties the rope connecting us to the dock. Just as he gets the last bit untied and begins to pull himself aboard, the woman who was once pursuing me leaps towards him. She grabs onto the railing on the side of the boat and attempts to pull herself on board.

My dad falls backward from the impact. Skylar runs to the railing and immediately pulls her leg up and stomps the woman forcefully on the fingertips of one hand holding her onto the boat. The woman growls and screams as she pulls her hand away from the boat, leaving herself dangling by the remaining hand.

I pull on the accelerator handle and take us away from the pier.

Dad gains his stability, stands up and, with the same motion as Skylar, pulls his leg up and kicks the woman's determined hand. She lets out a fierce shriek as her body falls along the side of the boat and into the water.

Skylar asks him, "You okay?"

"I'm good, now. Thanks, Sky."

My dad walks over and asks, "Want me to take over?"

"Yeah, I'm not sure what I'm doing, anyway."

"I figured. But hey, you found the accelerator."

I stand up and walk over to where Skylar is now sitting, looking back at the marina. I grab onto the railing to stabilize myself beside her, and she looks up at me.

"What would we have done if neither boat started?"

"I guess I hadn't thought about that. It wasn't part of the plan."

It was probably stupid to go into that situation so unprepared, but we really didn't have any other choice. I guess we could have jumped in the water and swam. But who knows if those deranged are able to swim, and who knows if that water was contaminated. We could have fought them off, shot them down, and given ourselves more time, but why waste the bullets when we don't absolutely have to.

"Do you want to sit down?" she says, charm illuminating her eyes.

I analyze her face and chalk this up to her attempting to make things go back to normal between us. Well, whatever normal may be, I don't want it. I put my wall back up between us and say, "No, I'm good," and turn my back as I walk away.

I catch her face slightly drop as I turn away and feel satisfied with myself as I push her away. Satisfaction soon turns to guilt. I don't want to hurt her, but she can't continue to lead me on. Until we reach the cabin, my goal is to keep my promise of protecting her, and nothing else. I promised to protect her—not her ego, not her emotions, just her. I have to remind myself that I can't continue to let her manipulate me.

As I walk back towards my dad, I look out onto the water. Beautiful, serene, peaceful. If I block out the sounds of the deranged growling at the pier, everything seems so placid. The sun has finally set, but a crimson red remains painted over the skyline, bleeding with hues of purple. The abundant forest around us provides a sublime backdrop for the burning sunset.

I grab onto the handle near my dad and assist myself into the seat opposite of him.

He asks, "Still want to go to the island?"

"Of course, why not?"

"Well, we've got everything we need here. We could just drop anchor and get a good night's sleep. I think there may even be sleeping quarters underneath."

"I still want togo, even if just for a few minutes," I say slightly let down.

"Okay...I mean, I figured as much. Kind of nostalgic, ya know?"

I say under my breath, "Yeah."

I look over my shoulder at Skylar. She's slumped over with her journal in hand, furiously writing away. She stops momentarily, sniffles, and then appears to wipe what could be a tear from her cheek.

Guilt courses through me as I realize I may have caused that tear and those frantic words. I do everything I can to add more bricks to the imaginary wall as I turn away and look the other direction.

CHAPTER TWENTY-TWO

SKYLAR: Sunday, May 24

I savor this moment of safety and embrace the wind blowing against my face. I put pen to paper, the only thing I know to do right now to soothe my soul.

I thought I could let him in, I felt he could maybe understand, to maybe work with me. I know it's crazy, it was one gesture, one thing. But he pushed me away. And it makes me realize I was right, he won't.

It's too much to expect of someone. Especially after what I've done to him. I continue to push him out, I always have...that wonderful self-preserving defense-mechanism...and I'm stupid enough to think that I deserve anything other than him pushing me out.

I wipe an uncontrollable tear off my cheek and hope they don't see.

I have to just let him go, to stop letting my guard down and hoping he'll come. I'm stronger than I let myself believe, I can do this. I will heal myself. I won't let the broken pieces bring me down. I'm scared, but I will overcome this.

I desperately wish for Wiley's safety. Part of me kicks myself for not taking off with Max in search of him. Keith would have murdered us himself if he knew. There will be another chance, there has to be.

And maybe there will be another chance for us, because something deep inside tells me there has to be, too.

CHAPTER TWENTY-THREE

MAX: Sunday, May 24

"Doing the cold shoulder?" my dad asks quietly.

"What?" I respond.

"It's like a game of cat and mouse with you two. Let me guess, you're the one pushing her away now?"

"It's not like that, nothing's like that," I stammer. "I mean—there's nothing there."

"Whatever you say, Max."

I roll my eyes as I choose not to respond. I hate how obvious things are to him. And I hate how oblivious things are to her and me. My side begins to ache; my head begins to throb. I'm hungry and thirsty, and fatigue has set in.

I open my backpack and grab a bottle of water. As I take a drink my dad says, "Oh, I almost forgot to tell you, we got a ton of stuff at the bait shop." He seems excited as he takes his backpack off. "Here, open it up."

He tosses me the backpack, and I unzip it in anticipation of what's inside. The fullness presses against the zipper and makes it a little difficult to open. A small, clear plastic package begins to poke out as I make my way around the backpack with the zipper. I open it wide and the package falls out. I chuckle as I realize my dad was excited about scoring a bunch of junk food.

I reach over and pick up the package that had fallen on the floor and read the side: Frosted Chocolate Mini Donuts. Inside the bag are numerous packages of candy bars, snack-sized donuts, potato chips, granola bars, crackers, etc. My eyes lock onto a hidden treasure at the bottom: beef jerky. While I'm not disappointed about the massive score of treats we acquired, I'm more satisfied with having something with protein and substance.

My dad says, "I know there's mostly sugary junk in there, but I grabbed all the trail mix and beef jerky that I could find. Skylar found a stash of canned soup and a few apples, so if we can make a fire, we'll be eating a warm meal tonight."

I look back at Skylar as she tucks her journal under her arm and sits there quietly staring off across the horizon. The deep reds and rich purples shimmering along the waters surface.

My dad adds, "She found a mini-fridge with some bottled drinks. I think she mainly grabbed the water and then whatever else would fit in her backpack."

I continue to look at her, mesmerized, until we reach the shore of the island. Her hair is pulled back in a low ponytail, and the loose strands flow with the wind as we cruise across the water. Her face is speckled with dirt and blood, and the swelling from her injury back at the train has just started to subside.

She raises a finger to touch her lips, pressed tightly in a line, just full enough to remind me of their inviting touch. She's gazing out over the water, and her eyes radiate pain, and passion, and fear. I'm struck by how her inherent beauty—subtle, but impeccable—falters under no circumstance, even when, no, *especially* when, she's being difficult.

We're coming up on the island now, and my dad says, "Let's leave our things here and make sure we're alone. Then we can figure out what's next."

I drop my backpack into the belly of the boat and observe the island from the rails. It seems smaller than I remember. I have to keep in mind that I was a lot younger, a lot smaller, when we came here before. I guess the island being smaller is a good thing now though, less ground we have to cover to make sure the coast is clear, literally.

I hop off the boat first, grabbing the rope to try to pull the boat closer inland. My dad follows and helps me pull it further. Skylar stumbles to the nose of the boat, looking uneasy. She kneels, and then sits down, dangling her legs off the front. I walk over and extend her my hand for support. She shuts me down and says, "I'm fine," as she jumps onto the ground on her own.

I realize the wall I put up may be a little smaller than the wall that she's returned against me. I think to myself how counterproductive we are. I try to get her to take down her wall, then I build up mine; then I let down mine, and she builds hers back up. I yearn for when we can actually have open communication with each other instead of constantly tearing each other down.

"Stick together or separate and go on each side?" I ask my dad.

"Won't take us long, let's stay together," he responds.

This is a better idea anyway. I'm getting restless, and I'm not sure I feel comfortable going off on my own, or letting him or her be alone either.

We make our way around the island quickly, being sure to

check most places we could access. The only thing we come across is a frightened rabbit, which runs off into the bushes. We head back to our boat and devise a plan of action.

"Let's gather some firewood and start a fire close to shore."

"Okay, you and Skylar do that. I'm going to grab what we need from the boat."

Skylar and I walk inland to gather some wood. I tell her, "Try to find some sticks, dry leaves or any logs."

"I think I know what to grab, Max."

"I was just helping, Skylar. I didn't know you were an expert fire builder."

"I didn't say I was. You just act like it's rocket science."

"No, I don't." I turn to her, irritated. "Go back up there if you don't want to help."

She looks at me with equal irritation and responds, "I'm *trying* to help, and you're treating me like a child."

I hear my dad holler, "Find any firewood yet?"

For a moment, we have a stand-off, giving each other angry blank looks until one of us decides to look away.

"Hello?" Dad again.

I turn away first, not because I was letting her win, but because I want to get this fire going so I can eat and go to sleep. I want this day to be over so we can be closer to reaching the cabin.

I gather as much firewood I can and make my way back to camp. I see Skylar and my dad already there, working on something. When I arrive, I see that they've made a divot in the ground and have begun spreading Skylar's gatherings.

My dad says, "I found a lighter in the cupholder of the boat. This should be a breeze." I drop my wood and sit down next to the pile. The log I grabbed was with the intention to scrape the innards out for kindling, so I get started on that with my pocket knife.

I rip the outside bark off of the log and peel back a damp layer, then take the knife and use it to scrape the inside of the log. I begin flaking the wood and then placing the tinder near the pit for my dad to use to start the fire.

After a few minutes of work, we have a successful campfire with plenty of spare firewood. My dad jury-rigs a makeshift holder on top of the fire so we can set our cans of soup on it without placing them in the actual fire. I'm disappointed when we don't have a can opener but then remember my knife. I drive it inside of the cans, one by one, and then hand them to Skylar and my dad so they can strategically place them above the fire.

We eat our dinner in silence until my dad asks, "Do you guys want to sleep down here, or in the boat? I think I'm going to sleep in the boat if you don't mind. I can pull the cushions out and make the bed if you want."

"I think I'm going to just stay down here, by the fire. I'll grab my sleeping bag and use some clothes for a pillow," I reply.

"What about you, Sky?"

She finishes her bite of soup and carefully responds, "I'll probably just stay down here, too. If that's okay? I'd be more comfortable near the fire."

"Good with me. I'm all finished so I can grab your sleeping bags." He walks away and then turns back as if remembering something. "Want any snacks while I'm up there?"

Skylar grins and says, "Surprise me."

My dad smiles back. "Deal! Max?"

"I'll have the same."

"Two surprises, coming right up," he responds giddily as he walks back to the boat. He grabs onto the handle and pulls himself up with ease.

I never realized the strength my dad has, both physically and mentally, until the past few days. He's been such a level-headed person through all of this. I'm so thankful for that, and that I'm with him—that we're both with him.

Remorse sets in when I realize Skylar lost the only family member that she's trusted, and it was my fault. I blame myself for getting irritated with her when she's pushed me away because she had every right to.

She's scared. She's alone. I wouldn't know how to handle things if I was put in her situation either.

My dad tosses us our surprise treats—her a Kit Kat and me a bag of peanut M&M's. I look up at her, and she almost reads my mind when she says, "Trade?" We toss our surprises through the air towards each other to swap.

My dad laughs and says, "Hey, beggars can't be choosers!"

Skylar says apologetically, "Thanks, Keith. I would have been fine with it, either way, promise!"

"Here's your bags. You guys good for the night? Just keep adding wood if you think it needs it. We should be good here until tomorrow."

"Yeah, I'm good. Goodnight, Dad."

"Night, Max, Sky. We'll be home tomorrow, okay? We're almost there."

"Night, Keith," she says as she forces a smile.

I grab one of the sleeping bags and unroll it. I walk over to Skylar and place the bag on the ground beside her. I walk back over and grab the other sleeping bag. I unroll it and stretch it onto the ground on the opposite side, a little further away from where I've been sitting.

I sit down and open the Kit Kat. I pop a stick in my mouth as I go through my backpack in search of a makeshift pillow. I find a couple of t-shirts and my sweatshirt. I ball up my two shirts and place them at the end of my sleeping bag and grab my sweatshirt, holding it out to Skylar.

"Here."

She gives me a puzzled look. "What?"

"Pillow."

"I'm fine, you can use it."

"Just take it, please."

I sense her analyze the situation as she hesitates. She slowly reaches out and takes the sweatshirt from my hand and says, "Thank you," in a tender voice.

I sit there for a few minutes eating the rest of my Kit Kat. I lie down and stare at the stars for a while. The sky is so beautiful from this point. The night is so dark, other than our campfire, and with not a cloud in the sky, every star is visible. I try to locate all of the constellations I can remember.

For a little while, I just stare, blankly, letting my mind have a break for a moment as I allow my body to relax, too. I shut everything out and begin to hear the pulsating beat from my head. I wonder if the aching pain will ever go away. I don't notice it as much when I'm occupied, but as soon as I try to relax, I realize it in full force.

I close my eyes and try to drift away. Even with my eyes closed, I can see the brightness of the fire begin to fade as it starts to dwindle down. Minutes go by. More minutes go by. I feel like I'm stuck in the in-between stages of wide-awake and total exhaustion.

I can't sleep. I'm exhausted, but I can't seem to shut my mind down enough to take me away. Then I hear something. I open my eyes and try to focus on what I'm hearing. It's her. I hear whispered sobbing.

I sit up and let my eyes adjust to the darkness before locating her beyond the fire. I see her, crouched in the fetal position on top of her sleeping bag. I try not to let myself think, to wonder why she's crying, or what I should do. I just get up and walk over to her.

I gently sit down beside her and then lie down. I feel her

tense up and take a deep, startled breath as I place my arm around her. I hold her for a moment and feel her whimpers start to dissipate. She turns her body slowly, to face me. She pulls herself closer and nestles her forehead against my chin. I deliberately press my lips against her forehead.

I assure her, "I'm here," and she responds by bringing herself even closer in my arms. I hold her tightly and focus on not letting her go. I close my eyes and imagine that if I can think about it hard enough, I could erase her pain. I feel her breathing regulate in my embrace as I fade away.

CHAPTER TWENTY-FOUR

MAX: Monday, May 25

I wake up to the sun beating down on my cheek. Skylar's face is still nestled against my chest, and for a second, I think I'm still dreaming. She has this constant effect on me when things are going smooth. She makes me feel as if I'm floating, but in the best kind of way. I don't want this to end.

I watch her breathe in and out just for a moment before I decide to ruin the perfection by getting up. My body feels stiff from lying on the ground, and the pain from my head and side begins to take over. I wiggle my arm out from under her head and gently place her face on my sweatshirt-pillow. She moves slightly but remains asleep.

I walk back over to my sleep station and grab the bottle of water from my backpack. I take a drink and walk to the boat to find the pain medicine. As I grab the handle to pull myself on board, my dad clears his throat and says, "Good morning."

"Morning, Dad. Hey, where's that Vicodin? Starting to feel it again."

"Let me grab it. We need to change those bandages on your side anyways. We should have done that last night, but we didn't really have the best lighting."

I sit down in the co-pilot seat while he rummages through our supplies to find what we need.

"Sleep well?"

"Once I was finally able to, yeah, like a rock. You?"

"Mmhmm. Boat was rather comfortable." He gives me a suspicious look and asks, "Skylar sleep okay?"

I stutter. "Ugh, I-I don't know, she's still asleep. Ask her yourself when she wakes up."

He brings the supplies over and tells me, "Lift your shirt." I do as he says and he continues. "I checked on the fire last night." While any other time I would think "good for you," I realize he's admitting that he saw our sleeping situation.

I reply with an open-ended "Okay..."

"Just wanted to let you know. So, you weren't trying to hide it like I didn't know. I think it's great. Of course, I would rather you two get along than fight with each other."

He takes the bandages off my side and says, "Gross," as he pulls away the saturated blood-soaked rags.

"Thanks," I say sarcastically.

"Sorry," he replies. "I just didn't realize you were bleeding this much, Max. You shoulda said something."

"I didn't know either. It's been hurting though, and so has my head. I don't notice it unless I'm not doing anything, but when I do, everything just throbs."

He stops for a second and fumbles around his bag. He pulls out the pill bottle and hands it to me. "See how many are left, and judge how much you want to take. We probably have over the counter stuff at the cabin but I'm not sure."

I look inside and see that there are only three and a half pills left. I decide to take one and leave the rest. I feel selfish if I take any more, not knowing if anyone else will need them. My pain isn't completely unbearable, it's just annoying.

He puts the supplies back in his backpack, and I give him a confused look. He responds with, "I need to clean your wound. It would be easier to do it down there and have you lean over."

"Oh, okay."

I follow him off the boat and hop onto the sand. I look back at camp and see that Skylar has woken up and is sitting on her sleeping bag, drinking from a bottle of water. I give her a half-smile, testing the waters, and she gives me a similar smile back.

We walk over to a clear spot and my dad says, "Go ahead and sit on your butt, and then I'm going to have you lean back on your elbows. Just go ahead and take your shirt off first."

I continue to do as he says and he continues to doctor me up. After a few minutes of soaking my side, he feels confident that he's cleaned it well enough to bandage it back up. He pats my wound dry and comments on how it's actually healing decent considering the circumstances. He finishes bandaging me up and says, "I would probably get a new shirt if you have one."

"Yeah, I do. Thanks, Dad."

I walk back to my original sleeping area, shirtless, and grab a t-shirt from my rigged-up pillow. As I pull the shirt over my head, Skylar asks, "Does that hurt?"

"I'll be fine once the pain meds kick in." I turn back to my dad and say, "Hey, don't forget about her face. You said you would check that out once we got stopped."

"Yeah, you're right, Max." He changes his path from the boat, back to the camp area to greet Skylar.

She tries to deter him by saying, "I'm fine, really. It's no big deal."

"It'll only take a minute. Just let me switch the bandage. We might not even have to put a new bandage on, just let it heal with nothing on it. Come here."

She inches towards him and looks away as he begins to take the bandage off of her face. I walk over and stand behind him as he works. With the bandage still on her face, the swelling appears to have reduced, but when he removes the bandage, I can see that the area surrounding the cut has turned a dark shade of purple. I cringe and she says, "It's really not that bad. It doesn't even hurt anymore."

"Now, now, don't be so modest," I say in fun.

She starts by giving me a little bit of her typical Skylar attitude but then lightens up and smirks back. My dad cleans her wound and then proceeds to apply a thin layer of ointment from the first-aid kit.

He says, "I think we should just leave the bandages off, unless it's bothering you."

"No, it feels better like this actually. Thank you, Keith."

"No problem. Now, how about you two quit getting hurt!"

"I can't help that I was born with two left feet."

"Think you can manage to at least grab some of our supplies and bring them back to the boat? Maybe kick some dirt on that fire without falling in?"

"Funny, funny, Dad. I think I can handle it."

After the fire is put out and our supplies are back on the boat, we decide to pay a little tribute to the island. We walk around for a few minutes, telling Skylar different stories about times long ago that we'd experienced here.

I think about the lunches my mom would pack us, and how much I miss her. I usually try not to talk about her too much because I know my dad was heartbroken over her loss. I couldn't imagine loving someone as much as my dad did my mom, and then losing her. My heart aches for the pain he must know.

We walk back to shore, where our boat is located and bid adieu to our beloved island sanctuary. I promise myself I'll come back here someday and tell my kids about the times my dad and I shared here, and maybe even tell them about this trip. I hope I have that chance.

My dad and I push the boat back off the shore. We aren't as far out as we'd like to be before hopping inside, but we don't want to risk getting too wet, not knowing about the water. Once inside, we start the boat and make our way away from the island.

In the daylight, I see that this boat is a lot nicer than I had anticipated. The upholstery doesn't even look like it's been used more than a few times. There is a little table in the middle of the seating section with fine polished redwood. In the front, the captain's seat is large with additional padding for extra comfort. And beside there, the co-pilots area has different control panels and about five cup holder areas.

This boat cost someone a pretty penny, and here we are cruising it around to save our lives. Many thanks to the rich bastard that bought this boat and left the key in the bait shop.

I look at the compass and see that we are headed southeast. My dad catches my eye and says, "Can't go wrong with this direction. We'll just go this way until we can't anymore, and then we'll find a decent place to hop out and go on foot."

"Sounds good to me. Hungry?"

"Yeah, good idea. Fuel ourselves up before we go back out into the real world."

After we finish eating, we cruise to the farthest section of the lake. We all stand at attention while surveying the land we're approaching. We arrive near a dock, to try to make our departure as smooth as possible. We slow down just before we arrive and scope out the area before making our final descent.

After a few moments go by and we see that the coast is clear, we cruise in. We've already packed all of our supplies and stand with our backpacks on. We decided the sleeping bags would no longer be of use, so we leave them behind. Guns all loaded and ready for action.

My dad recognized that we'd be crossing over a state route so we need to take extra caution in choosing our path. When we reach the pier, I jump onto the dock first. I grab onto the rope that he tosses me and help steer the boat in. My dad cuts the motor and lets the boat's momentum cruise itself in.

We reach a stopping point, and my dad follows me onto the dock. While I tie the boat to the dock, my dad helps Skylar off. I look over as she jumps onto the dock with his help and can't help but feel as if I should have been the one to help her. I guess I've been taking it upon myself to protect and help her, and I feel like I should have done this now.

My dad says, "Let's move. Edge of the park isn't too far this way," as he motions to the trees. "We'll be most covered there, and we'll be able to see the road before the road sees us."

We make our way towards the wooded area as we fall into our normal formation. I keep my eyes peeled as we creep by, tree by tree. They're quite beautiful this time of year—when the dingy winter emptiness is replaced with summer's blossoms. It reminds me that through any amount of darkness, things can change, you can be whole again.

We've been walking for about thirty minutes when I hear the first noise that startles me. My dad hears it simultaneously and falls back to assess the situation. We crouch down and make our way towards the noise.

We hear people, muffled people. When we finally get close enough, we see a small group of men standing in the distance, at the road intersection, manning what appears to be a road-block. We look at the far sides of the opposite highway and don't see any activity.

My dad nods for us to fall back. When we get a little farther away, he says in a softened voice, "I think they're only at the intersections. If we can cross up there, as quickly as possible, we may be able to sneak past them."

"Yeah, I mean that's our only option, right?"

"Right."

My dad looks to Skylar and I follow suit. Her face is pale, and she looks unsure of the circumstances. She quietly clears her throat and says, "Whatever you guys think."

"I want us to move fast and stealth-like. We'll take it easy getting to the edge of the trees, but once we hit the pavement, get your butts in gear. We don't want to draw any attention to ourselves, but we can't just mosey on across. Follow my lead, okay?"

Skylar and I both nod, and although I would rather call the shots, my dad's confidence makes him appear like he knows what he's doing.

We make our way a little farther into the woods to get away from the intersection while moving towards the road at the same time. We hit the edge of the tree line and assess the surroundings before moving on. In the far distance, we can see the roadblock and hear the echoes of the chatter. We look to our left and neither hear, nor see anything.

My dad nods and I know this is it, time for action.

At first, we move slowly, assessing what kind of impact our presence has. When we reach the pavement, we quickly glance both ways. Nothing in our immediate vicinity. As soon as my dad's foot hits the pavement, he takes off running with such ease and secrecy. Skylar takes off after him, and I follow behind her. My legs are inherently faster than hers, but I choose to slow myself and maintain our normal arrangement.

We pass two lanes in a matter of seconds and begin on the final two. My dad reaches the grass first and begins to make his way across a yard. As I turn to my right, to the men in the distance, I'm alarmed when I see them making their way towards us. I hadn't heard them start their vehicle, or maybe perhaps it was already running.

I urge to Skylar, "Faster, NOW!"

CHAPTER TWENTY-FIVE

MAX: Monday, May 25

I pick up my pace and quickly hit the grass. I head toward my dad and see him turn to the men. They're coming toward us. He changes his path and heads in the direction of the house. Without any words spoken, Skylar and I follow him. We make our way to the front of the house and continue to run around the backside. My dad catches me off guard when he grabs my arm from behind the house when we run past. I hadn't realized that he stopped running. I look at him questionably and he presses his finger to his lips to indicate to be quiet. He takes the same finger and points toward our previous path.

There, about a hundred feet away, stand two people, a man and a woman. They lack typical human behavior, which implies they may have been infected.

Skylar whispers to my dad, "What do we do?"

I reply, "Let's head west and cut through that alley."

"And if there are people there?" my dad asks.

"We've got guns." I continue, "We'll cut back over out of the men's way as soon as we get far enough away from those deranged."

My dad begins to move and I cut him off. "I'll take the lead, you take the rear."

He gives me a look of irritation at first but then lets me pass him. I pull my gun from the holster and aim it ahead of me. We make our way covertly to the alley. Houses envelop us on both sides, and I grow uncertain of what will be waiting for us at the end. This is our only option, we have to make it work.

Our backs are up against the house as we make our way through. I'm a few feet ahead of Skylar when I reach the end. I motion for them to hold positions as I check out what is waiting for us. I look outside and see nothing but a peaceful neighborhood. I make my way to the house on the other side and turn to assess. I confirm that we're clear and have them come to my side. I begin to speak and am silenced when I hear the sound of a vehicle reaching pavement somewhere around us.

I decide in a split second that we need to move, we can't be sitting ducks.

I say, "Follow me," as I take off running. I don't think, I just run. I know that if we're moving, we might be one step closer to safety. We dodge sheds, run by porches, hop over fences.

We keep moving.

We keep moving until I see a field in the near distance. My dad has caught up to me by now and motions for us to stop. We shield ourselves behind the last house as we catch our breaths. My dad says, "I think we've lost them. The men, and the deranged. I'm honestly not sure if either of them had ever known we were there, but we didn't let them find out." He pauses for a moment and says, "Good job, Max."

"Do you know where we are?" I ask my dad.

"Sort of. I'm pretty sure there are a few houses on the other side of those trees." He points at the gap between the trees and us. A cornfield stands between those trees and us. The field has already been planted and the corn stands about a foot tall.

"And that's where you wanna head?"

"It's our best option."

Skylar says, "I agree. At least we're going in the direction we need to be, right? We should be able to see behind us and ahead pretty well."

"All right, let's head straight for the trees."

Without saying anything else, we take off towards the trees. It takes us about five minutes to make our way across the cornfield to the closest section of trees. I feel relieved when we reach them. I've always found comfort in the woods. Maybe it's how peaceful things seem to be, maybe it's just being away from the city. It's pleasant—being able to hear yourself think, and smell the fresh, unrefined air.

I feel even more relieved that we're closer to *our* woods, our sacred place in the middle of nowhere. Our hideout, our safe haven. I know once we get there, I'll feel safe again. My dad has stocked up enough firepower, food, and all the other resources we need to stay off the grid. If it weren't for the locals, I'm not sure anyone would even know we had a place out there on that chunk of land. To be honest, for all they know, we just go out to an empty property.

When I was younger, I remember helping my parents install solar panels on the property. I always wondered why they did this, and now I'm thankful for them, whatever their reasoning. I know the world won't fix itself once we reach the cabin, but I know that we'll be able to at least find safety and figure out what to do next.

"So, what do we do now?" Skylar asks.

"Same thing we've been doing. We'll take the trees as far as we can, keeping hidden. Then we'll scale past these houses.

Maybe we can find some wheels. The further we get away from the city, the better we'll be. I doubt there's much manpower ahead of us."

"And what if you're wrong?"

"Would you rather stay here, Sky? We're doing the best we can to get home," he replies with growing irritability. "And before you ask, I don't have a plan past getting home. That's my plan right now, and that's all I'm concerned about."

Skylar stutters, "Keith, I—ugh, I didn't mean to upset you." She puts her head down, almost ashamed for the response he gave her.

"I'm fine, Sky. I just really want to get where we're going. I don't see why we can't make it there before nightfall. Maybe sooner if we can find some type of transportation."

I interrupt. "Well, how about that?" I point to an old Chevy truck parked next to the barn at the house we're approaching.

My dad grins. "And there we go. That might actually work, if it runs!"

The truck sits about thirty feet from the barn and is surrounded by a patch of overgrown grass all the way around. I assume that the truck was parked and then grass grew around it. I begin to lose hope that we'll be able to get it running. The majority of the truck is a pale blue but covered in brown and red rust. The two, round headlights seem to be intact. On top of the wheel wells sit the round, yellow blinkers. The tires seem to have air pressure even though the truck sits low to the ground. As we approach, I see an ax and rope in the bed of the truck.

I reach towards the door handle and remember that we should probably assess our surroundings first. I draw my hand back and say, "Want to make a quick sweep before we start making noise?"

My dad answers, "You and Sky want to while I mess around with the truck? Kill two birds with one stone?"

Skylar nods so I reply, "Yeah, deal. C'mon."

She walks around the side of the truck to meet me. We begin walking and I tell her, "Go ahead and get your gun out. Just have it in your hand in case we need it. Leave your finger off the trigger unless you're ready to shoot."

"See, this is what I'm talking about, Max. Immediately you start treating me like a helpless child. Did you forget who saved your ass when you got all pissy and left the house?"

"Right, sorry. You just act so...uneasy, with the gun."

"I just don't want to use it unless I have to."

"Well I'm here, so hopefully you won't have to."

We check out just far enough to feel comfortable and then make our way back. I figure there's no point in going too far and stirring up any unwanted attention if we haven't already. The deranged only seem to really notice us when we're loud or in direct view. As long as we can sneak back, get the truck running, and be on our way, we should be good to go. I wonder how fast can they run?

I noticed a few times that they are hesitant at first, and then often start sprinting. I assume they can't run any faster than a normal human, but maybe just don't react to being winded. The woman at the boat screamed when we hit both of her hands. I assume that was from the pain, but could have been the aggravation of not getting to us. Do they just want to beat us up?

I think back to the old lady at the bait shop. So, she must have been what the emergency broadcasters called comatose. From what we saw, those just go completely dormant and then slowly die? I'm surprised that she was the only one we've seen so far, but maybe the others are still inside their homes, or maybe we passed them but didn't even see them.

I wonder if my dad was right about the deranged becoming less active at night. There is so much to think about. I try to shut my mind down and file away all of my blistering questions until we can get to safety.

We get close to the truck, and my heart begins to race when I see no sign of my dad. I turn to Skylar and share a fearful look with her as we take off running towards the truck. Before I go into full panic mode, my dad's partially salt and pepper locks appear from under the dash of the truck. I see his head through the windshield and force myself to calm down. I place my hand on the handle of the old rusty door, and it squeaks as I open it.

I say to my dad, "Make any progress?"

"Give me about two seconds and we'll see."

One...two...

I hear the faint sound of the ignition and the motor trying to come to life.

"Okay, two more seconds," he says in an amusing tone.

My heart palpitates when I hear the sound of the motor.

My dad peeks his head out and says, "Ta-dah!"

Skylar and I both allow a slight chuckle as we make our way towards the passenger side of the truck.

"Good job, Dad."

I kick the weeds down around the truck door and reach for the handle. I firmly push the button with my thumb but have no success in opening it. I quickly realize the door is locked. I tap on the window to signal to my dad to unlock the door. He stops fumbling under the dash and stretches as far as he can to pop the unlock button. With the tip of his fingers, he's able to pop the lock and then subsequently fall. He hits his face on the gear shifter and instantly puts his hand to his mouth.

I open the door and peek my head in to ask, "You okay?"

He lifts himself up with one hand and holds his mouth with the other. When he takes his hand away, I see blood on his mouth and coating his hand.

I laugh and say, "Wonder where I learned to fall so gracefully?"

He smiles a bloodstained smile and replies, "Got me there."

I open the door the rest of the way and motion to Skylar to get inside.

She smiles and says, "Thank you, sir," as she takes my hand to assist herself in sitting down. She slides her way to the center of the bench seat as my dad tries to clean himself up. I slide in after her and close the door behind me. As I get adjusted in my seat, my knuckles graze her bare-skin knee. I feel a flush run over my body as I pull my hand back.

I stack another brick on top of the wall I hold between us and push away the feeling of desire she provokes in me. My dad gives a thumbs-up and pulls the door shut behind him. He pushes in the clutch and slides the truck into gear. He slowly releases the clutch while giving the truck gas. The truck hesitates but is persistent.

I wonder what this truck has seen, being so old. I wouldn't mind keeping it if we can make it back to the house. It appears to be in pretty decent shape, considering the age, and that it's been sitting out in a field. I can't believe it's still running. I'd want to come back here and buy it though. Well, if the world is ever back to normal, that is.

We take off, sputtering our way through the yard of the truck's legal owner. I stare out my window at the emptiness around us. We close the gap between the house and us and make our way towards the driveway.

I ask my dad, "Are we taking the roads?"

"Should be able to take side streets and dirt roads. I'm putting my money on them only pursuing the main roads. You know, the highways, state routes..."

Skylar's eyes widen so I tap my hand on the hand that she

has resting on her leg to assure her that we'll be okay. I brace myself to keep the wall strong and not let any feelings through.

"The only place I'm worried about is Tarlton. We've got to head through there to get home. There isn't any way around that. I doubt there will be any officials there, but I can't imagine the city will be vacant."

"Well," I say, "we've got guns. And we can't give up this close. Tarlton is what, like ten minutes from the cabin?"

"On a normal day, yeah. But we'll be fine." He gives his best situational smile trying to make us feel hopeful.

"It's wicked hot in here," I say as I begin to crank the window down.

We turn onto the road, and as I'm rolling down my window, I look back at the house and see a person opening the front door. I continue to roll down the window as the person runs towards the end of the driveway waving their hands through the air. Our truck picks up speed as the person begins to become just a blur in my vision as we distance ourselves. I see the blur make its way back towards the house before I lose it in my vision completely. A pit forms in my stomach as I become uneasy about what just happened.

CHAPTER TWENTY-SIX

MAX: Monday, May 25

I feel something brush my face and when I turn back from the window, I see Skylar's hair blowing in the wind. She instantly says, "Sorry," as she begins to tuck her hair behind her ears.

I smile and say, "It's fine, really."

She smiles back as she continues to tuck her hair back and locks her eyes with mine. We share a split second of bliss before she looks down and then looks away. My heart beats faster, and I throw another brick on top of my wall.

We speed up to what seems like around 50 mph, but with the broken speedometer we're unsure of the actual speed. The roads are desolated and deserted. Houses we pass are vacant and seem tenantless. Occasionally, we pass a house with a deranged person nearby. When they hear us, they take off running toward us momentarily, and then quit running when we get too far away.

We don't obey the traffic laws.

We haven't stopped for stop signs, or used our correct lane. Periodically, my dad will instinctively use his turn signal when turning onto roads. I laughed the first two times; now I think he does it on purpose just to be funny and lighten the mood.

We continue to drive for the next fifteen minutes with ease, occasionally dodging road debris or slowing down to make a turn. I feel relieved knowing we've covered so much ground in this truck, safely. I really don't mind the on-foot adventure, but risking our safety not knowing what's out there isn't very appealing.

And it's not just my safety—it's Skylar's safety, too. My dad continues to prove that he's able to endure whatever's thrown at him, but she continues to have self-doubt and signs of weakness. Skylar struggles with her own mind; I've seen her be strong, and I've seen her break down. Not that I'm perfectly capable, I just try to not externalize it as much.

I glance over at her, her hair blowing in the wind. The sun beams through the windshield, reflecting off her cheeks. She looks frozen in time, but still moving. I want to keep her frozen here, to protect her, to disallow her fears from impairing her. I want to help her overcome her weaknesses and to fuel her strengths. And I want her to want that for me, too. I know deep down that's what she wants, but she continues to push me out. It must be fear, that she's afraid of letting me in.

I want in. *Please just let me in, Skylar. Tell me what to do.*

My heart aches, and my mind tries to telepathically urge her to have faith in me.

We begin to slow down as I see a city-limits sign up ahead.

My dad says, "Okay, time to get our game faces on." I have to lean into Skylar as I reach behind myself to pull out my gun. I apologize as I check to make sure my gun is loaded.

She asks quietly, "Should I get mine?"

My dad responds as he pulls his gun out, "Here, hold onto mine now. I'll take it back if we need to use 'em."

She takes his gun and cycles a bullet into the chamber. We drive towards the sign slowly and read: *TARLTON Population of 285*. My mind flashes back to the tiny village of Lockbourne, when I was forced to shoot that little girl. I try to shove the horrible, guilt-covered memory back into its hiding spot.

The abundance of trees lining the road obstructs our view of the town. We won't know what waits for us ahead until we've gone too far. But, we have no choice—this is our only way unless we backtrack to another city, a bigger city with bigger unknowns. We cruise down the road with ease as the tension inside the truck begins to grow. I see Skylar's knees start to bounce up and down, so I shoot her a quick glance to help her calm down. If I had it my way, I would pull her into my arms, and shield her face from whatever we're potentially about to see, so she wouldn't have to fear.

We round the corner, and I swallow hard in anticipation. I see the small town up ahead. Old houses line the majority of our path, along with a bank and a few other local businesses. A gas station waits at the end of the road. We need to get past that gas station, and then turn right. Once we make that happen, we should be able to pick up our pace and make our final stretch home. Optimism is so close; we just have one more hurdle to jump.

We initiate our expedition through the city. I look across the truck to catch my dad's eyes.

He says, "Looking good," with a buoyant expression. I start to feel more secure with each inch farther into the city. I look down alleys, into front windows. There's no sign of life. I wonder where all these people have gone. Are they hiding—did they seek refuge elsewhere—were they taken—are they dead? So many questions come to mind as I scan the area.

We pass an old ice cream shop, and I immediately recall it from my childhood. My mom had taken me there on our way to the cabin. She would get a twist ice cream cone, and I would get plain chocolate. We would sit out on the picnic table in front of the shop and eat our ice cream together. She always made the smallest situations seem like such a special time. I miss her, specifically for those moments.

I stare blankly out the window, holding on to the memory of my mother as I hear Dad say, "Up there."

I'm quickly brought back to reality as I turn that direction and see them. At least half a dozen deranged swarm the parking lot of the gas station. I become alert and say, "Let's keep going. We're so close to the next road."

"That's the plan. I'm just going to cruise, try not to draw attention to us. So far, they haven't seen us. I'll step on it when we're about to pass."

Please, oh please, just let us get another three hundred yards. I reposition the gun in my hand, and Skylar shows her concern by starting to bounce her knee again. She looks down at the gun in her hand momentarily and then up at me. I don't give her the smile she was looking for because I don't want to give her false hopes. She turns away and looks at the group ahead.

As we just about get to the point of acceleration, I notice something peculiar. I see the deranged pursuing a person—a sane person. My dad has already taken his eyes away from the group and begins to push on the gas when I reach across and grab his arm.

"Stop!" I shout.

"Max, we're clear!" he responds back.

"We have to stop, there's a—there's a person! They're chasing after a person, Dad. We have to stop."

As he turns to look, I grab onto the door handle and open the door.

"Stop, Max," Skylar persists.

"Keep the truck running. Roll up the windows."

Before they can stop me, I hop out of the truck and take off toward the gas station.

CHAPTER TWENTY-SEVEN

WILEY: Monday, May 25

I wake suddenly to the sound of gunshots... somewhere inside the building. *Shit.*

My heart starts to race. Sweat begins to bead and roll down my face. *Shit, shit, shit.*

I don't want to die here.

I open my eyes wide but all I see is darkness. The door to this room is closed. I hear people running down what I assume to be the hallway, and the occasional gunshot sometimes followed by someone screaming out in pain.

I swear it seems like I sit there forever, just listening to the chaos unfold and running different scenarios through my head, concluding every time that I'm going to die.

This is the part where my life is supposed to flash before my eyes, right? Then why is it that all I can think of and see is my impending death.

I don't know how long I've been here, maybe a day or two.

The "nice" doctor came in to tend my wounds on different occasions and would take the restraint off of one arm to allow me to eat. It surprisingly wasn't bad, the food. Same sandwich every time, no matter breakfast, lunch or dinner. Now that I think about it, it was probably to confuse me on the time.

Twice they fully unrestrained me and let me go to the bathroom, which was inside the room I've been held in. Multiple guns to different areas of my body and the threat that they would kill me made sure I would just use the facility and go right back. Unfortunately, on occasion, I couldn't wait.

The "mean" person that came with the doctor just wanted to beat me around and ask questions I had no answer to. I swear, I really would tell him if I knew something. I'd give anything just to end this torture.

He doesn't give too much, just asks where the rest of the resistance is, which I told him it was just my family and me. We're not much of a resistance.

In between questions, he would threaten to hurt me, then actually land a few punches. The doctor would usually intervene and stop it before it became too unbearable. The interrogations typically ended after I'd either blacked out or was sedated. Both of which I welcomed.

Another gunshot brings my mind back to reality as I realize how loud, and close it was. The doorknob creaks slowly, different from the sudden turn of my normal visitors. I freeze. I think I even hold my breath.

The light switch makes a click and instantly I see brightness. I don't make a sound. The figure comes closer and I can't help myself, I close my eyes. I close them so tightly.

I feel something unfamiliar, a finger against the back of my head underneath the blindfold, pulling it away from my eyes. I keep my eyes closed.

"Open your eyes," a stern voice commands.

Shit.

I slowly open my eyes, they ache with the fullness of the light, something I haven't truly seen in too long.

Before they can adjust, he speaks again. "Who are you?"

I clear my throat, "No one, please don't kill me."

I see him, finally see him and it takes me only a second to recognize his face.

It was only a few days ago we stole a UTV from him.

"Sanchez?"

He looks puzzled, "How do you know my name?"

I begin to explain and apologize for what we did.

He continues to look over his shoulder at the door, not much gunfire, just the occasional man yelling out, "All clear!"

A man enters the room and says, "We're secure, entire building."

Sanchez lowers his gun and holsters it, and then reaches for a knife attached to his belt. He points the jagged blade at me and says, "This was not us—we did not do this to you—we are part of the solution, not the problem."

"Wait...wha—"

He cuts me off. "I'm going to cut you free, please stay calm. I want you to know that everyone else is dead, so if your family was captured with you, they're gone. We can take you to our safe house."

He cuts the zip ties that have been digging into my body and relief floods me.

I start to cry. "Oh God, are you serious? Is this a trick? Please, shit..."

"No, sir, not a trick. Now just come with us, we'll get you to safety."

"Wa—wait, Skylar, Max... no, Keith, scientist, super smart, Jesus he's brilliant, engineer... Dim—"

He cuts me off again, "What?"

I take a deep breath and regain my composure. I continue to wiggle my free arms and legs to get all the blood flowing and admit that I must look like a complete idiot.

"Sit still, what are you saying?"

I start slowly, telling them who I was with, and then all at once, how we were escaping, to get away but also to regroup, and Keith was sure he would be able to figure something out.

"You're talking about Keith Sinclair, DimChem?"

"Yes, you know him?" I start to feel uneasy.

"Yes, he's exactly what the resistance needs."

My eyes must have bugged out, because Sanchez cracked a smile and hit my bicep with a playful punch and said, "Come on, let's go find your family."

CHAPTER TWENTY-EIGHT

MAX: Monday, May 25

As I get closer, I see the person they are chasing. She's a young girl, probably my age. I run towards them as they run towards her. They haven't even noticed my presence in their obsessive pursuit of her. She becomes trapped and is forced to climb on top of the roof of a dark-blue SUV.

She climbs onto the hood, and one of the deranged grabs onto her ankle. She screams and kicks the person in the head, freeing her leg. She climbs her way on top of the roof and regains her footing. The deranged start shaking the SUV and pounding the windows and doors with their fists. The sounds of growling and groaning fill the air.

I cower behind a gas pump as I take my first shot. I hit one of the deranged in the back, and he falls to the ground. I take another shot and miss, shooting the driver's side door. I see the girl begin to frantically look around, trying to find the source of gunshots. I quickly scale the station and make my way to the next closest pump.

By the time I can aim for my next target, one of the deranged grows curious and begins to head my direction. I shoot directly at his chest and bring him to the ground. Five more deranged swarm the SUV. I see a gap arise where four of the deranged start to walk to the far side of the SUV. I appear from behind the gas pump and aim my next shot straight at the one in the way.

I motion with urgency for the girl to jump and say, "Now!"

With only a momentary lapse, she decides to trust me and jump. She starts to run towards me, and as she does, the deranged notice that their prey has relocated. They take off running behind her, and just as she reaches my side, I'm forced to take another down. Four left. I grab her arm and take off running toward the truck with her. I hear the sounds of angry footsteps behind me, and while barely looking, point my gun behind me and shoot. I know I've made an impact when I hear one of the deranged screams out.

I point ahead and say, "There. Get in there!"

We reach the truck at the same time and jump in the bed.

I holler, "Go, go, go!"

When I turn around, I see three, and a partially slower fourth, continuing their quest towards us. I hear grinding as my dad tries to get the truck into gear. I begin to breathe heavier and grow anxious as I see the deranged closing in. The motor sputters and throws us backward.

One of the deranged reaches us just as we take off. She leaps toward the truck and grabs onto the trailer hitch. I unsteadily move my way toward the tailgate, and before I can remove her, we hit a large pothole, forcing her to lose her grip. I reluctantly sit back down and put my gun to my side and my head in my hands.

The truck accelerates, and I know we're in the clear: we made it.

After a moment, I look up and see the terrified girl sitting across from me. Her rosy cheeks are tear-streaked and her dark brown hair is partially stuck to her wet face. She's petite, but possibly taller than Skylar. She looks familiar, but I can't figure out where I know her from. I let myself assume that she's close to my age, within a year either way.

I feel guilty that I haven't already acknowledged her.

"What's your name?"

"Quinn."

I watch as her hands shake, and I'm unsure if the cause is the rattling of this old clunker as we speed down the road, or the fear she exudes.

"Are you hurt?"

"No, I mean, I don't think so, I uh..." her voice trails off and her eyes begin to wander.

I clear my throat. "Why were you there? You could have been killed."

She locks her eyes with mine. All I see is apprehension; she doesn't speak. I continue to look at her, assuming she would speak, but she doesn't.

I hear a noise against the back window of the truck and see my dad reach back and bump the glass again. Through the window, I hear him say, "Gonna stop soon."

I feel the truck slow down as we start to stop. There is no point in pulling over, so my dad just stops the truck in the middle of the road. Farm fields surround us, with the closest building not even in sight. I brace myself as I stand and I offer Quinn a hand to do the same. Skylar and my dad open their doors and climb out of the truck.

"You two okay?" he says to us.

I look at Quinn and back to my dad. "Yeah."

My dad extends a hand to Quinn to help her over the tailgate and out of the truck bed.

"There someone we need to go back for, sweetie?"

She looks away and then to the ground, and says, "No."

"Let me get this straight, you were out there all by yourself? Bit of a suicide mission."

"I, uh, didn't start out alone. But, now I am. Well, I mean when you found me."

She hesitates, "My family...the people I was with, I don't have anything to go back to."

Silent tears begin to stream down her face as she continues to look at the pavement between her feet. I don't know what else to do, so I place my arm around her shoulder and try to give her a reassuring grasp. She turns, quickly, towards me and begins sobbing into my chest. I place my other arm around her and pat her back as I tell her, "It'll be okay, you're okay now."

Skylar clears her throat unnaturally loud, and I turn my attention to her. Her mouth is in a straight line and her eyes almost pierce through me. The already loose grip I had on Quinn dissipates, and irritation begins to course through me.

"What?" I say to Skylar.

"Nothing," she barks back.

I take a step towards Skylar. "No, you're not going to just say 'nothing.' What do you intend on starting a pointless fight about now?"

She looks down.

I take another step forward and ask again, "Skylar?"

She looks up at me and repeats, "Nothing," and turns her attention to my dad.

"Not the appropriate time, you two."

"Oh, and when is it ever the appropriate time with us?" I respond hastily without taking my eyes off of Skylar.

As she begins to walk away, I walk toward her and take

hold of her arm. "Let's take a walk," I say gently but with conviction.

"Max, seriously, not now. We need to figure out what the hell we're doing," he pleads.

Quinn speaks up. "I should leave, I'm sorry, this is my fault. Thank you, for...back there."

I turn my attention to them as I walk away with Skylar, "No, you two stay right here, this will only take a minute."

When we get out of earshot, I take my hand off of Skylar's arm and with a gentle voice I say, "Will you talk to me now?"

"It's not important, Max." She crosses her arms.

"Skylar, you have to tell me something, anything? You're killing me with this up and down shit."

She looks up at me, and with tears forming in her eyes, I know she isn't going to respond.

"I can't do this," I say with the smallest voice. "It doesn't have to be all or nothing, just give me something."

She continues to not speak and the frustration inside me builds.

My voice grows louder. "What do you want from me, Skylar? What do you want me to do?"

I take a breath, and continue. "There's nothing more I'm terrified of than the way you make me feel, good or bad."

I pause. "Answer me! Please! Why can't you answer me?"

She doesn't answer.

"I'm done."

I raise my hands to my head and grip my hair as if I'm going to yank it out. I let out an irritated grunt as I forcefully throw my hands down to my side. As I begin to walk away I reach back and start dropping the things I've been carrying, figuratively, and literally. First, I let my backpack slide off of my shoulders and hit the ground.

I hear my dad in the distance. "*Max, what the...!?*"

I keep walking. I shake my head, and keep walking.

I've lost what's worth fighting for and grow sick as I realize I don't think I ever had it anyways.

Her voice pierces through me. "Max, stop."

I keep walking.

I hear footsteps behind me and then feel her as she grabs onto my arm. I pull away and she says, "Stop, right now."

I stop, turn around, and this time, I'm the one who doesn't speak.

"Don't do this, Max."

I don't say anything. I just peer deep into her eyes and try to read her. The deepest part of her soul, to her exterior, I don't think I'll ever figure out, but I don't have the will to quit trying.

"You can't leave," she says unconvincingly.

I stare at her beautifully bruised face and say, "Then you need to give me something, anything."

She reaches down to grab onto my hand, and raises it to lie against her cheek. She presses her hand against mine and closes her eyes as the warmth of my hand is transferred to her already warm cheek. She opens her eyes slowly and the desperation she once exuded is replaced with longing. She takes her free hand and reaches up to my face. She stands up taller, and onto her toes as she pulls my head towards hers. I lose sense of reality as I take my slack hand and wrap it around her waist to pull her upward, and into my embrace.

We kiss.

And in this moment, eternity with her doesn't seem long enough. Every problem I once had temporarily disappears and I'm lost with her.

I am hers, she is mine, at least in this moment. And I'll take it, because, at this point, it's all I can get.

I can't deny that things are far from resolved, but I know

she cared enough to give me this, my something I begged for. And I'll take it.

She slowly pulls her lips away from mine and lingers for a slight moment before I let her body touch the ground completely. I don't say anything, not because I don't have words, but because I know nothing needs to be said right now.

"Let's go," she whispers.

As we reach my dad and Quinn, he sarcastically says, "You two lovebirds done now?"

I glare at him and he continues, "I'll take that as a yes. On to more pressing matters though. Quinn here doesn't have anyone to go back to. Well, that she knows of their whereabouts. So, for now, we've decided that she's staying with us. I know this won't be an issue, right guys?"

I look at Skylar out of my peripheral and see her face tense a little. She quietly says, "Right," and I nod my head in agreement to satisfy my dad's probably rhetorical question.

"Alright then, back in the truck. At this rate, we should be able to make it to the cabin before sundown. Max, I want you in the bed for lookout, okay? And I assume Sky, you'll join him. Quinn, you can ride in the cab with me." He points at each of us when he says our names. "Chop chop," he barks as he makes his way toward the truck. The presence of his authority is welcomed, and I'm appreciative of someone else assembling the plan.

I look up before walking to the truck and see a few storm clouds approaching. The smell of summer rain caresses my senses, and I'm reminded of my childhood at the cabin. I can't count how many times I ran around our property, playing in puddles and getting muddy when I was younger. My mom would usually yell outside and tell me not to make a mess, but would always smile and laugh about how dirty I would be when I finally came inside. I smile just thinking about her kind but carefree attitude.

I climb into the bed of the truck as Quinn and my dad are settling into the cab. I give Skylar my hand and help pull her inside of the bed with me. It's a hard feeling to shake, that voltage every time my skin touches hers. I wonder if she experiences it, too.

The truck starts, and after we remove our backpacks, we sit opposite of each other beside the wheel wells. Our legs fully extended, side by side. The truck begins moving and we're closing in on our final destination. Finally.

The humid wind meets my face, and I feel my overgrown hair flow with its tempo. I can't help but look at Skylar, being this close to her. She yawns. And I motion for her to come to me. She smiles gently. As she climbs towards me, we hit a bump in the road, and she loses her balance. I grab onto her to give her stability, and we gently laugh when we hear my dad holler from inside the cab, "Sorry!"

She turns around and puts her side toward my chest and rests her head against my shoulder. She leans into me, and I wrap my arms around her to hold her close. I gently kiss her forehead and as I do, I close my eyes and breathe this moment in. These moments with her seem so temporary. I have to take in every bit while I can.

She brings her knees forward, and places them against my thighs. Through the ever-changing movement of the truck and the sound of the engine, I feel her exhale. With each moment, I become more susceptible to her every being.

I'm yours, Skylar Morgan, I'm yours. I ache for you to know this.

I close my eyes and breathe in the warm, thick air. I fight to keep this moment as I begin to drift away. I want to keep it. I need to keep it.

CHAPTER TWENTY-NINE

MAX: Monday, May 25

Everything happened too fast. Our moment. The road. The mud. The water. *Her.*

It should have been simple.

I awoke to the sudden, and constant, jerk of the truck. Instinctively, I reached for my backpack—for my weapon. My eyes quickly fixated on my dad, with his arm and head hanging out of the driver-side window as he pushed on the accelerator.

"Stuck!" he shouted.

"Yeah, I got that," I replied. "Why exactly are we in the field?"

"Bridge is out, must have been that downpour from last week."

"How convenient," I mutter sarcastically.

He slams the truck into park and shuts off the engine. He grabs his backpack and throws it into the bed of the truck. He says, "Look out, incoming!" after he already tosses it back. I hear him snicker under his breath.

"Quinny, throw yours back, too. And then climb back."

Great, he's already got a pet name for her, too. I can't help but roll my eyes. I hope for everyone's sake that Skylar didn't hear that, too.

They climb into the bed of the truck and we all decide continuing on foot is our best—and only—option. It seemed simple really, or it should have been. My dad had driven us halfway through the field in an attempt to get us as close to the cabin as possible. He failed miserably when he got the truck stuck in a relatively vast amount of mud. There really was no way around it on foot. We all tried our best, but no matter where we got out of the truck, into the mud we went.

Maybe we were becoming delusional, or maybe it was the fact that we were so close to the cabin, but we couldn't help but laugh. We made it this far, and now, we were wading through shin-deep mud closely approaching our destination. I grabbed Skylar's hand and allowed her to use me as a crutch. My dad followed suit and extended his hand toward Quinn(y).

"Thanks," she said shyly.

"What's that sound?" Skylar said nervously.

"Good ol' nature, Sky," my dad replied. "Should be a creek just ahead unless I've lost my bearings and don't know where we are."

"No, you're right," I chimed in. "Right over this crest." I pointed towards a small hill with my free hand. "The cabin is about three hundred yards on the other side of the creek."

"Other side, like, we have to cross a creek?" Skylar asked.

"Yeah. No biggie. Hey, it'll help wash all this mud off," I reply lightly.

When we reach the top of the crest, Skylar drops my hand almost as simultaneously as I drop my jaw.

"Hope you kids can swim," my dad says.

As many long weekends and summers that I'd spent here, I'd never seen the water this high, or this violent.

"It's only about a hundred feet across, maybe." I try to reassure Skylar, while trying to reassure myself. "I'll be right there with you."

"Are you kidding me? Seriously? You think we're just going to wade through *that*."

"Yes, seriously, unless you have a better option."

"Well, no. But, it doesn't look safe."

"Neither does hanging out like sitting ducks until a drought," my dad says. "Let's do this."

He starts down the hill towards the creek first and motions for us to follow. I grab Skylar's hand and give her a gentle nudge to get her moving. Quinn doesn't say much. She looks pained, but with just enough determination to continue. She follows my dad closely with cautious steps.

From here, everything becomes one big blur of a rapid moment. We all went into the water, one after another, in groups of two. It was cold at first—maybe because it was so hot outside—but became warm within seconds. Things seemed to be going fine. The grip Skylar had on my hand was taut. I could sense her uncertainty, her unease. I led; she followed.

Once we reached what seemed like the middle, I began to struggle to keep my footing and my head above water at the same time. I knew she couldn't touch the bottom. We were almost there. The water began flowing harder, thicker, and faster than before. I felt branches and rocks brush past my face and my torso.

That's when it happened.

I felt her hand grip tighter right before I lost it. I heard her scream right before I heard nothing. I turned as fast as I could to see her right before she went under. I didn't have time to process, I just reacted. I dove into the waters behind me, toward her. I frantically swam with the current, reaching, grabbing, grasping towards anything.

That's when I felt her. I grabbed onto her limp arm and pulled her and myself to the top of the water. I grabbed onto her waist and used every ounce of what I was taught in third-grade swim class to get to the other side. As I reached the shore, I felt hands pulling us. My eyes focused on my dad and the nothingness I once heard was filled with his voice.

"Max, what hap—Oh my God, Sky. Quinn, help, now." It was all a blur of noise.

Tunnel vision. All I could see was her. The fresh blood running out of her already bruised temple. The sinking feeling in the pit of my stomach because I couldn't keep her safe. *I just wanted to keep you safe.*

My dad had already ripped her backpack off. He was pumping his crossed hands into her chest and plugging her nose to breathe into her mouth. I was frozen; I couldn't react. Fear swept across me quicker than I could have imagined. I sat, dumbfounded, for what seemed like eternity as my dad continued to perform CPR on her.

That's when she came back to me. With one swift pump to the chest, life was restored in both of us. I snapped back to reality as she began to sit herself up, while coughing up the water that had been filling her lungs. I reached towards her, and she reached towards me. Then she reached up and placed her hand on her head, where the blood was coming from.

"Ow," she muttered.

I hadn't noticed my dad already got the first-aid kit out and was searching for a bandage.

"Here, this oughta do until we get the rest of the way," he said as he placed a makeshift waterlogged bandage across her brow. "You okay to walk?"

"Yeah, I—I think so," she managed to say. "Just, give me second."

When she was ready, I helped her to her feet. She didn't let go of my hand. Her grip became tighter than before, and she stayed closer than ever. She didn't speak. I thought maybe she might be in shock. She was wobbly, but I expected it, considering the circumstances. I just held her tight and tried to support as much of her weight as I could without completely carrying her.

I struggle to find the words for how I felt when I saw that cabin. That cabin was home; it was safety. And we finally—and I mean finally—got there. This cabin would be our safe haven. It would be the place where we would gather our bearings and figure out what to do next. Now that the world had basically gone to shit, we would have to regroup, and this is where we would do it.

For a second, I felt as though I could breathe easier. *We made it.*

But, only for a second.

"I need to rest for a moment," Skylar said quietly as she put her hand down to support herself as she sat down on the stairs of the cabin's front porch.

I helped her down, and sat beside her. "We can go inside. I can help you get to a bed. What do you want me to do?"

She looked up at me, and I knew immediately something was wrong. Her eyes, which are typically full of such radiating beauty, were dull, and bloodshot. Her face was pale, and the bloodstained bandage on her brow was a vibrant shade of red.

"Is it your head?" I asked her. "Dad, hey, come here, now," I said to my dad as he was finishing putting our backpacks in the front room. I hadn't even noticed that he had opened the front door, and Quinn was already inside.

"No, I mean—yeah, but I-I just, I just don't feel...right."

My heart sank, for what felt like the millionth time in the past few days. More than a few scenarios crossed my mind. I looked at my dad, with what must have been complete fear, because he immediately said, "Max, get her in the house, now." His tone was serious, and it made me even more fearful.

"C'mon, Sky. Up," I said as I stood up and tried to pull her weight up, too.

"I-I can't. I feel...so...heavy."

My dad rushed over and grabbed her other side, and helped me pull her up. I picked her up and cradled her as I felt her body begin to go limp. I carried her through the doorway. I could feel her face, right next to my neck.

She mouthed, "I'm scared."

"Shh, I got you. It's gonna be okay. You're gonna be okay. We're gonna be okay." At this point, I didn't know who I was trying to reassure—her or me.

I rushed back to my old bedroom, the closest room with a bed, and laid her down. I brushed the golden, and water-mangled piece of hair out of her face and looked into her eyes. They somehow managed to become more bloodshot in the last thirty seconds. She looked at me, with those dull, and aching eyes and said, "I'm just so—so, tired."

"Stay."

I put my hand up to her face. "Of course, I won't leave you." My heart tightened in my chest.

Her eyes began to shut slowly, and with her last ounce of strength she said so softly, almost mouthing, "I need you."

My heart was so full, but yet so broken in the very same moment. How could I ever let this happen to her?

I pressed my lips to her forehead as I squeezed my eyes tightly shut, one single teardrop falling out.

My dad was right there, pulling me back. "Max, let me in. I need to see her." Everything began to blur together again. I felt another hand on my shoulder. It was small and delicate. I hadn't heard her speak in a while.

"Max, hey, give your dad a little space," Quinn said with ease.

"Just do something. *Dad*, do something. What's wrong with her?" I pleaded.

"Max, calm down. She's here. She's still here. See. Look for yourself."

He had a blood pressure cuff around her lifeless arm. "I don't know what that shit means."

"It means she's here. Her blood pressure is low, and so is her pulse, but for now, she's here."

"You have to do something. Dad, you *have* to do *something*."

"I know, Max. We'll do everything. Right now, you just need to calm down."

ACKNOWLEDGMENTS

I want to thank:

My mom for the endless love and support.

My dad for letting me live in his basement.

My tiny human for all the sweetness.

Ninja, for giving me all the fur cuddles and loving support through some of the hardest years of my life; I will forever miss you.

All the friends and family that cheered me on along the way and shared and purchased my work. Especially those that read my book in its many drafts and gave me great feedback.

Victoria for being my go-to "please help" friend.

Veronica Roth, for making me cry for three days straight and inspiring me to be a writer.

And lastly, you, for giving my writing a chance to be read; I will be eternally grateful.

ALSO BY KATE MYERS

The Comatose - The Deranged Series Book Two

A deadly virus. A girl who suddenly falls ill. And a boy who would risk it all to save her.

Max Sinclair should be enjoying the summer following his high school graduation, but instead he's dealing with the aftermath of a rapidly spreading bio-weapon gone wrong.

Getting safely to their cabin off the grid was all Max and his companions had in mind, but now, they're frantically trying to figure out how to save Skylar—the girl he finally got back after all these years.

When an unlikely guest fills the group in on the truth behind the epidemic, Max and his father struggle deciding who to trust, especially with his dangerous secret.

Will Max be able to do what it takes to save the girl he loves and keep his secret safe? Or will he succumb to the virus in his attempt to do what he thinks is right?

The Comatose is an action-packed young adult dystopian romance that's full of daring choices, sacrifice, and fighting for what you love.

Want to learn a little more about fan favorite Keith Sinclair? Grab a copy of The Consequence on Amazon, or join Kate's newsletter to get a copy for free!

The Consequence - Prequel

The Deranged - Book One

The Comatose - Book Two

ABOUT THE AUTHOR

Kate Myers has been writing fiction since 2013. She obtained a bachelor's degree in accounting and business, only to realize writing was her true passion. Kate does her best writing when she's drowning in coffee and not distracted by cats. She is an avid reader and book lover, young-adult fiction being her favorite to read and write. Kate lives in small-town Ohio. When she's not writing (or reading), you'll probably find her making endless to-do lists that she will either lose or never complete. The Deranged is her debut novel.

Kate also writes new adult paranormal romance under the pen name Luna Pierce, and contemporary romance as Tessa James.

 facebook.com/sorryforthekate
instagram.com/katemyersauthor

www.ingramcontent.com/pod-product-compliance
Lightning Source LLC
Chambersburg PA
CBHW061617100726
47898CB00002B/702